My First Story

Middlesex

Edited by Jenni Bannister

About this book ...

First published in Great Britain in 2012 by:

Young Writers

Remus House
Coltsfoot Drive
Peterborough
PE2 9BF
Telephone: 01733 890066
Website: www.youngwriters.co.uk
All Rights Reserved
Book Design by Ali Smith
© Copyright Contributors 2012
SB ISBN 978-0-85739-936-6

Welcome!

Young Writers was established in 1991 with the aim of encouraging writing skills in young people and giving them the opportunity to see their work in print. As a part of this imprint, My First Story was designed for Key Stage 1 children as an introduction to creative writing and to promote an enjoyment of reading and writing from an early age.

The simple, fun storyboards give even the youngest and least confident writers the chance to become interested in literacy by giving them a framework within which to shape their ideas. As well as this it also allows older children to let their creativity flow as much as possible, encouraging the use of imagination and descriptive language.

We believe that seeing their work in print will inspire a love of reading and writing and give these young writers the confidence to develop their skills in the future.

Our defining aim at Young Writers is to foster the talent of the next generation. We are proud to present the resulting collection of regional anthologies, containing the first stories from our authors of the future.

CONTENTS

Hambrough Primary School Southall

Kenyngton Manor Primary School Sunbury on Thames

Northwood College
Northwood

Orley Farm School
Harrow

St Michael & St Martin's Catholic Primary School Hounslow

St Michael's CE Primary School Enfield

Imagine ...

Each child was given the beginning of a story and then chose one of five storyboards, using the pictures and their imagination to complete the tale.

The Beginning ...

One night Ellie was woken by a tapping at her window.

It was Spencer the elf! 'Would you like to go on an adventure?' he asked.

They flew above the rooftops. Soon they had arrived ...

MAGICAL ADVENTURE

Storyboard 1

JUNGLE TALE

Storyboard 2

PIRATE ADVENTURE

Storyboard 3

SPACE STORY

Storyboard 4

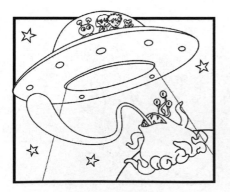

Zoo Adventure

Storyboard 5

The Stories

Alma Primary School
Enfield

Lauren's Zoo Adventure

They went to a zoo. They went through the door and they saw an elephant.

The elephant took them around the zoo, they found bamboo.

They found a panda and baby panda.

The elephant took the people to see the monkey.

They ate bananas and swung on vines and they had fun.

Spencer elf took her home, she said, 'Goodbye.'

Lauren Vaughan (7)
Alma Primary School, Enfield

Filiz's Zoo Adventure

Ellie and Spencer went to a zoo.

They played with the elephant.

They played with the panda.

They played pirates on the elephant.

They ate bananas with the monkey.

They went home.

Filiz Hakyemez (6)
Alma Primary School, Enfield

Nehir's Zoo Adventure

At the zoo a very friendly elephant greeted them at the door.

The friendly elephant gave them a fun ride to see all the friendly animals.

Then they met panda and her baby. Spencer picked up the baby panda.

Friendly elephant then gave them a ride to see the gorilla.

Friendly gorilla shared a banana with them. Ellie was happy.

It was the end of the beautiful adventure with Spencer and Elephant. Ellie waved at them both and said, 'Goodbye.'

Nehir Temur (6)
Alma Primary School, Enfield

Anil's Zoo Adventure

The girl and the boy went to the zoo.

Then they sat on the elephant's top and found it such fun.

They both played with the bear.

They walked around in elephant's top.

The girl and the monkey ate bananas.

The boy left the girl in her house then the boy went.

Anil (6)
Alma Primary School, Enfield

4

Farah's Zoo Adventure

Spencer and Ellie went to the zoo and they were watching an elephant. Ellie was holding a teddy bear.

They both were riding the elephant who was holding the teddy bear.

Spencer was holding a teddy bear, the big panda was holding baby panda and Ellie was holding the big panda.

They went back on the elephant again. He was holding the teddy bear.

Ellie came down from the top of the elephant and she started eating bananas with the monkeys.

Spencer was still riding the elephant. He was saying goodbye to Ellie and she was saying goodbye to him.

Farah Ward (6)
Alma Primary School, Enfield

Suad's Zoo Adventure

At a zoo with lots of animals, they stepped inside and they saw an elephant.

They climbed on the elephant and the elephant picked up with its trunk a baby panda. The elephant gave the baby panda to Ellie and Spencer.

And they sent the baby panda to her mother.

After they sent the baby panda back to her mother they explored more of the zoo.

Then they saw some monkeys and they ate a lot of bananas until it was midnight and it was Ellie's bedtime.

They said goodbye and they went home.

Suad Abdirahman (6)
Alma Primary School, Enfield

Naufi's Zoo Adventure

Once upon a time there was a fairy called Jake and he took a girl to the zoo.

They rode elephants.

They hugged a baby panda and a big panda. Then they rode an elephant home but they got stopped by a giant monkey.

They all had a banana and set off back home at midnight and went to bed

Her mother was very worried. The little girl was very happy to be home.

Naufi Mustafiz Zara (6)
Alma Primary School, Enfield

7

Belmont School
Wealdstone

Zaphaneth's Space Story

They flew into space.

The alien saw the girl.

They got taken by an alien ship.

They had a ride.

They got attacked by an alien.

She got a ride back home.

Zaphaneth N Buertey Puplampu (6)
Belmont School, Wealdstone

Hardik's Space Story

Soon they were on the moon.

They went in the spaceship.

The alien monster came.

The alien dropped the little girl at her home.

Hardik Hirani (5)
Belmont School, Wealdstone

Ayub's Magical Adventure

It was a lovely day. There was a boy and a girl. They had a lovely pony. Their pony was beautiful. They were riding in an adventure.

They met an angry dragon. It was very angry. They were so scared. The dragon was breathing fire.

The children were running as fast as they could. They were so very scared even the teddy bear was running fast.

They sat on the pony for a ride. They were so much happier they went on an adventure. It was a big adventure.

They met a kind witch. They were sad, very sad. The bear got a lollipop. The bear was happy but the children weren't happy.

The witch gave them a magic broom. They were almost going home. Ellie was happy.

Ayub Hamid (6)
Belmont School, Wealdstone

Celine's Magical Adventure

One sunny day the children went for a ride. It was sunny and the trees were shaking.

On their ride they saw a dragon, he had fire in his mouth.

They ran and the dragon followed them.

They rode their horse and they were safe.

Suddenly the witch came with her broomstick.

Then they went on the broomstick and they went home safely and sound.

Celine Katjal (6)
Belmont School, Wealdstone

Mohamed's Magical Adventure

When the sun arrived the beautiful horse stopped.

They met a dangerous dragon. The dragon blew fire, *roar!*

The elf and the girl ran and ran.

They went to another land.

They met a witch, the witch was sneaky.

They went to a nice place.

Mohamed Houfel (7)

Belmont School, Wealdstone

14

Naeima's Magical Adventure

They went to a beautiful land. They went with a unicorn. They were riding on the unicorn.

They found a big green breathing fire dragon he was scary and spiky.

They both ran away from the dragon. They all said that was scary.

They went somewhere else.

They met a witch. They thought the witch was nasty.

The witch gave her broom so the children could go home.

Naeima Zaman (7)
Belmont School, Wealdstone

Sohail's Magical Adventure

Spencer and Ellie had a beautiful ride when the sun came.

Then there was a dangerous dragon.

The dragon breathed his fire then Spencer and Ellie ran as fast as they could run.

Then Spencer and Ellie went up and up before they reached the unicorn.

Then they saw a magic witch.

The witch said, 'Hey, you meddling kids!' The teddy hit her on the face with the lollipop.

Spencer and Ellie got the witch's ride and took Ellie home. It was night.

Sohail Mohammad Karimi (7)
Belmont School, Wealdstone

16

Zahi's Magical Adventure

When the sun was coming they arrived on a beautiful beach. A clown fish came out of the water.

Suddenly a horrible fire-breathing dragon came. The fire-breathing dragon was going to get them.

Spencer and Ellie rushed away from the horrible dragon. The dragon was still breathing fire.

Then the colourful unicorn came back to take the kids. The children were so pleased with the unicorn.

They saw a bad witch. They were a little bit scared of the bad witch.

They took the witch's broomstick and flew back to Ellie's colourful and beautiful house.

Zahi Ihsan Mohamed (7)
Belmont School, Wealdstone

17

Jvonne's Space Story

Ellie and Spencer were flying to space.

Ellie and Spencer were collecting stars and an alien was looking at them.

Ellie and teddy got taken by the alien.

Ellie saw all of the stars.

Ellie and the alien got scared.

Then they dropped Ellie home.

Jvonne Morgan-Burgher (5)
Belmont School, Wealdstone

Mawada's Magical Adventure

Tilly and Spencer got on a beautiful nice unicorn.

Suddenly they stopped; they saw a big horrible green dragon. They got scared.

They ran and ran so they could be safe.

They got on the unicorn again.

Suddenly they stopped, a wicked witch was there.

They went on a flying broom. They flew back home.

Mawada Najem (6)
Belmont School, Wealdstone

19

Layla's Magical Adventure

Ellie and Spencer rode on a horse.

They were scared when they saw the dragon.

They ran away from the dragon.

The horse saves them.

They met a witch.

The witch took them to their house.

Layla Jones (5)
Belmont School, Wealdstone

Iustin's Pirate Adventure

Ellie and Spencer were in a boat.

They found a treasure chest.

Ellie and Spencer met a pirate.

The pirate took them to his ship.

Two dolphins helped them get away.

Ellie and Spencer went home.

Iustin Tucaliuc (5)
Belmont School, Wealdstone

Ieshurun's Zoo Adventure

Ellie and Spencer went to the zoo.

Ellie and Spencer were riding on an elephant.

Ellie and Spencer played with the animals.

Ellie and Spencer went through the zoo.

Ellie and Spencer get with the animals.

Ellie had to go home.

Ieshurun Levi Nistor (5)

Belmont School, Wealdstone

Adnan's Space Story

Spencer is taking Ellie to space and Ellie is smiling.

The alien wants to take Spencer and Ellie is pointing to a star.

The alien is taking them in the spaceship. Ellie is worried.

Ellie is waving and the alien is waving too.

They get stuck in some mud, they are really scared.

Ellie is saying bye to the alien and Spencer.

Adnan Wahabdeen (5)
Belmont School, Wealdstone

Baieravi's Magical Adventure

'This is what I found last time I came,' said Spencer.
'Cool,' said Ellie. 'Let's go on an adventure.'

The unicorn took them to a magical land. They walked for some time. Soon they saw a horrid dragon.

'Quick, let's run away,' said Teddy. They ran for their lives.

The unicorn took them somewhere else, that was a magical place too.
'I can't wait,' said Ellie.

Soon they arrived. They walked for a minute. They saw a wicked witch.
'Eat these lollipops,' said the witch.

They bought a broomstick.

'Let's go home,' said Spencer. Soon they arrived home.

Baieravi Kohulan (6)
Belmont School, Wealdstone

Nova's Magical Adventure

'Wow,' said Ellie, 'A unicorn!'

'Yeah,' said Spencer the elf.

'Oh no, a fire-breathing dragon! What are we going to do?'

'Quick, run! We need to get back to the unicorn.'

'Phew, that was close. The unicorn already came.'
'That was a very wicked witch.'

'Want to eat a lollipop?'
'Sure.'

Finally they went back safely into the dark night at home.

Nova Jude Shrestha (5)
Belmont School, Wealdstone

25

Kierra's Magical Adventure

Ellie was asleep and Spencer knocked on the door and he said, 'Let's go and have a very magical adventure.' When they got there they saw a unicorn.

When they got there they got off the pretty magical unicorn. They met a big dangerous ferocious fire-breathing dragon.

Then the dragon breathed out hot orange fire out of his mouth and Ellie, Lilly the teddy and Spencer ran as fast as they could.

Then they jumped onto the unicorn and flew away and they passed fields, flowers and trees.

Then they met a nasty witch and she said, 'Have a lollipop. But they are very poisonous and they might sting you.'

Then they stole the witch's broomstick and took off to fly in the sky back home.

Kierra Joseph (7)
Belmont School, Wealdstone

Amaar's Magical Adventure

'Look at that unicorn, it's so shiny.'

'Look what I can see, a dragon it's breathing fire.'

'Run away before it breathes fire at you.'

'Come on; let's go before the dragon gets us.'

A witch! 'Go on take one sweet but be careful, it's poisoned.'

Finally we arrive home. 'Thanks, let's go on that adventure again.'

Amaar Abdallah (7)
Belmont School, Wealdstone

Hadia's Magical Adventure

Once upon a time there was a girl and a boy and they were really happy and they were playing with the unicorn. They had lots of fun.

Then there was a dragon and the dragon blew fire at the children and the children were scared.

The children ran from the dragon and the teddy ran.

Then the unicorn came back to the children and they were really happy.

Then a witch came and gave some lollipops and the children were really scared.

They ran away with the broomstick to their home.

Hadia Wakil (6)

Belmont School, Wealdstone

Rayan's Magical Adventure

Two children are on a unicorn. The unicorn is standing with two legs. There is a tree with one eye.

There is a dragon with sharp teeth. He is in a bad mood. The two children are very scared of the dragon.

The two children are running away from the dragon. The dragon lets out fire.

The two children went back to the unicorn and jumped on its back. The unicorn galloped away.

The two children saw a wicked witch. There were flowers that were lollipops.

Then they went on the witch's broomstick and went back home.

Rayan Mohamud (6)
Belmont School, Wealdstone

Bourne Primary School
South Ruislip

William's Pirate Adventure

Holly and Tom went on an adventure to Desert Island.

On the island Holly found some treasure. Tom saw a pirate ship on the sea.

The pirate came off his pirate ship and he was angry because Holly and Tom found his treasure.

The angry pirate said, 'Come on my ship.' Then he made Tom and Holly walk the plank.

The friendly dolphins heard the pirate's cannon fire and came to the rescue.

Then their pirate adventure was over, they went home for tea.

William Docherty (5)
Bourne Primary School, South Ruislip

Lucas' Pirate Adventure

It was summer and Jack and Ellie went on a boat on an adventure.

They saw an island and searched for treasure. 'There's a pirate ship,' said Jack.

'Hey, leave that treasure girl! I am Captain Nasty and it's mine forever!'

The pirate took them to his ship to walk the plank.

Suddenly two dolphins came to rescue them. Ellie saved her teddy.

It was midnight and Jack and Ellie were still going home.

Lucas Roberts (6)
Bourne Primary School, South Ruislip

Lucy's Magical Adventure

Once upon a time Lucy and Harry went for a ride on their unicorn.

Then they met a dragon. It roared at them.

Harry said, 'Run Lucy!' And they ran as fast as they could.

At last they found their unicorn, jumped on and ran some more.

Then they met a witch, they were very scared.

But they managed to escape on her broomstick. They were safe at home.

Lucy Rose (5)
Bourne Primary School, South Ruislip

34

Tallula's Magical Adventure

Once upon a time there was two children and a teddy, they rode on a unicorn and met a fierce dragon.

They were on the way and the unicorn's hooves went *clip clop*.

Until the unicorn stopped in front of lollipops.

They walked for a while, then they met a witch.

They nicked her broom.

They flew home.

Tallula Burton-Ward (6)
Bourne Primary School, South Ruislip

35

Amy's Magical Adventure

Once upon a time there was a little girl called Amy and a little boy called Harry. They lived with their pony called Sally.

One day they saw a dinosaur, they were very scared. He could breathe red and orange fire.

They ran with their teddy Bob, Harry and Amy ran so fast that the dinosaur could not catch up.

'Yes, he did not catch up!' Harry and Amy got on sally and set off again.

They met a witch, she said, 'Can I have a lolly?'
'No, no!' said Harry and Amy.

'Let's go home, it's getting dark. I'm freezing,' said Harry. So they went home and lived happily ever after.

Amy Sitton (7)
Bourne Primary School, South Ruislip

Adam's Space Story

One day a boy and a girl went to the moon.

An alien called Noname caught them. He took them to his planet.

They were terrified. They did not know what to do.

Anyway, he was nice. He took them to their planet.

A very bad monster saw them, he tried to get them.

Then they went home and lived happily ever after.

Adam Bielak (7)
Bourne Primary School, South Ruislip

Rohan's Space Story

Jack and Jill went to space to visit aliens.

When they went there they were playing on the moon.

But the alien lifted them into a spaceship.

Then they made friends but one ship was firing.

When it was time to go home they saw a monster with a long tongue.

Finally they were home.

Rohan (7)
Bourne Primary School, South Ruislip

Paul's Pirate Adventure

Once there were two children named Rob and Jack and they were sailing across the sea.

They ended up in a secret island and found some treasure.

When they opened the treasure box a pirate appeared called Captain Black Teeth.

Captain Black Teeth sent them to his ship and told them to jump into the sea.

Suddenly they jumped but some dolphins caught them.

Then they went home happily ever after.

Paul
Bourne Primary School, South Ruislip

Amelia's Magical Adventure

Once upon a time there lived a brother and sister called Joe and Amelia. One day they went and had a ride on their unicorn.

Suddenly a gigantic dragon came out of nowhere. He breathed out fire, they nearly got burnt!

They ran and ran until they got to where they both started.

When Joe and Amelia were back on their unicorn they rode off to a cottage made of sweets.

Suddenly a witch came bursting out of the door saying, 'Come in, come in, it's lovely.' She was a quite nice witch.

When they were in they straight away wanted to go home so they grabbed the witch's broom.

Amelia Green (6)
Bourne Primary School, South Ruislip

Ali's Space Story

Once upon a time a boy called Blue Eye and Hand wanted to go to space.

They landed on a planet and searched for aliens.

They met some aliens who said, 'Blah, blah, blah,' and they couldn't understand them.

Both of them had spaceship and went to speed off.

They took each other home and said goodbye to each other.

Blue Eye and Hand came back and Mum felt comforted.

Ali Ahmad (6)
Bourne Primary School, South Ruislip

Josh's Space Story

Tom and Joe were flying in space.

Tom and Joe landed on another planet called Sog.

Then a good alien came to help them to go back to Earth.

They got lost in space!

They landed on a strange different planet with hungry aliens.

The alien took them back to Earth and said goodbye.

Josh Seers (6)
Bourne Primary School, South Ruislip

42

Gabriella-Rose's Magical Adventure

Once upon a time there was a magical place which had a magical pony. There were kids who rode on the pony.

Suddenly they heard a roar. They knew who it was, it was a dragon!

They quickly ran until the dragon blew his fire out. They nearly got burnt.

Next they found their pony but they saw one evil witch and her house was made out of sweets.

They saw the evil witch. The evil witch told them they could come in but the evil witch lashed at them.

And they saw a piece of string and they easily got out.

Gabriella-Rose Anstey (6)
Bourne Primary School, South Ruislip

Earlsmead Primary School
Harrow

Biraven's Space Story

There once lived a girl and a boy who went to space to find the Earth.

Then there was a cheating alien who saw them and the alien was trying to put them in his space machine.

The alien just picked the girl up on the space machine.

The girl and the alien became friends. The boy is friends with the alien too.

When they were friends they accidentally got a gummy three-eyed alien.

Finally they dropped the girl at her home.

Biraven Inparasa (6)

Earlsmead Primary School, Harrow

46

Amina's Magical Adventure

Once upon a time there lived a pony, a girl and a boy; they were going to a magic show.

When they got there a scary dragon came along and scared them with fire.

So they ran away with a teddy. The girl lost her shoes.

They found their pony and ran away, far away. They didn't know where to go.

They found a witch, they asked for help from the witch.

She gave them a broom and teddy held on tight.

Amina Mohamed (6)
Earlsmead Primary School, Harrow

Isaiah's Jungle Tale

They were swinging on the vines.

And then they found a snake and they were a bit scared.

Then they ran away.

They met a lion.

And they rode on the lion's back.

And then they went back on the vines.

Isaiah Manderson (5)
Earlsmead Primary School, Harrow

Abivarja's Magical Adventure

Once upon a time there lived a pink unicorn and Sam and Rose. They had a lovely teddy bear.

Then they went shopping. Suddenly a fire-breathing dragon blew fire to Sam and Rose, they were scared.

They ran as fast as they could but Rose left her teddy bear.

Then a lovely pink unicorn came and rescued Sam and Rose and then they were happy.

Then along came a kind witch and asked them, 'Do you want to ride on the stick?'

Sam and Rose were excited and they lived happily ever after.

Abivarja Sivakumar (6)
Earlsmead Primary School, Harrow

Vishayini's Magical Adventure

Once upon a time came a dragon.

He scared two people.

The children ran away, the dragon chased them.

Then the children jumped on a unicorn.

Then they jumped off the pony.

They flew away on the way they saw a house.

Vishayini Balasubramaniam (7)
Earlsmead Primary School, Harrow

Ayeesha's Magical Adventure

There once was a colossal unicorn who was pretty.

Then there was a fierce dragon, they were scared.

The fierce dragon chased them, they ran as fast as they could.

The unicorn saved them. Then they went to her house.

Then a magic wizard came and frightened them.

The wizard took them home on a broom.

Ayeesha Patel (6)
Earlsmead Primary School, Harrow

51

Mithusha's Magical Adventure

Once a boy called Jack and a girl called Lucy and a horse called Dponey met a scary dragon.

They were frightened.

They ran away from the scary dragon and the teddy bear was fast enough.

Then they went on the horse to be safe.

Later they saw a lollipop and they got it.

Finally they got home with a broomstick.

Mithusha Sakthitharan (6)
Earlsmead Primary School, Harrow

Sahil's Space Story

Once upon a time a boy and a girl were in space.

There was an alien watching them.

Then the alien took the girl.

The alien still had the girl. The alien was attacking the boy and the boy was attacking the alien.

Then the boy rescued the girl.

After, the boy and the girl came back home.

Sahil Juya (6)
Earlsmead Primary School, Harrow

Sangeerthan's Space Story

Once there lived a boy and a girl, they lived in a colossal space planet.

One day they took some very special stars. An alien saw them taking the stars.

The alien took the special girl but not the boy and they took the teddy.

The boy took his ship and came to rescue but the alien wasn't bad.

He let the boy come in the ship. Suddenly a monster came; they were riding the ship so fast.

They went home. The girl went home but the boy didn't because it was such fun in space.

Sangeerthan Wijyakumar (7)
Earlsmead Primary School, Harrow

Hambrough
Primary School
Southall

Mathushan's Pirate Adventure

I went with my sister in a boat for a sail in a full moon day.

We saw a big box full of gold coins. We jumped with joy!

A pirate came and opened the treasure box with magic. Inside the box we saw lots of valuable jewels.

We took the treasure box and went in the pirate's boat and reached the island.

We sat on the dolphins and we played in the water, it was fun.

Me and my sister came with my dad from the seashore. This was the end.

Mathushan Manoharan (5)
Hambrough Primary School, Southall

Anshpreet's Pirate Adventure

One day a boy and a girl go on a boat trip on a sunny day.

The boy and girl found treasure and the girl was standing on top of the treasure.

A mean pirate wanted to take the treasure.

The mean pirate was making the children scared. The children jumped into the ocean.

Luckily two dolphins saved the boy and girl.

It was night-time; the children reached safety and were now going home.

Anshpreet Singh (6)
Hambrough Primary School, Southall

Saran's Pirate Adventure

They were sailing down the sea and they were going on the island.

And then they saw treasure.

A pirate came along and said, 'Get away from this treasure.'

The pirate said, 'Come along on my pirate ship and go home.'

And then when they were going home, two dolphins arrived and set off home.

Then they arrived home and had the best trip ever.

Saran Kirupakaran (6)
Hambrough Primary School, Southall

Akshaja's Jungle Tale

Once upon a time there was a girl and a boy going to the jungle.

They saw a snake and they got scared, especially Dashna.

They ran away from the snake.

They found a kind lion but felt a bit scared.

The lion, named Joseecern, rode them out of the jungle.

They want home.

Akshaja Thangeswaran (5)
Hambrough Primary School, Southall

Abeeha's Magical Adventure

Once there was a girl and a boy riding on a unicorn.

Suddenly a monster came and scared them away.

Then they ran away from the monster.

Then they again sat on a unicorn.

After they met a witch.

The witch gave them a broom. They sat on it and went back home.

Abeeha Riaz (5)

Hambrough Primary School, Southall

Benny's Magical Tale

One day Benny and Clara went on a unicorn for a ride.

Suddenly a dragon came and scared them.

Benny and Clara and the little teddy, Ashly, were frightened and began to run.

Benny and Clara got on the unicorn and were riding home but they got lost.

Suddenly a witch appeared and gave them a sweet.

With the witch's broomstick they flew home and lived happily ever after.

Benny Sathiyaraj (5)
Hambrough Primary School, Southall

Simran's Magical Adventure

One day Jake and Jill went off with their unicorn in the forest for a ride.

The unicorn got lost and they found a dragon.

The dragon blew out fire and scared Jake and Jill.

Jake and Jill found their unicorn and played.

They met a witch.

They took the witch's broom and went home.

Simran Kaur Bal (6)
Hambrough Primary School, Southall

Murad's Space Story

One night Jack flew Ella up in the sky far away from Earth. The stars looked very bright.

On the moon Jack showed Ella how to hold stars. An alien was standing laughing at them.

The alien got his spaceship and zapped Ella and her teddy into his spaceship.

Ella had so much fun; she even made an alien friend.

The mean monster tried to suck the spaceship but it was too fast and it got away.

After a great adventure Jack dropped Ella home before sunrise.

Murad Khan (6)
Hambrough Primary School, Southall

Sarpreet's Magical Adventure

One sunny morning Jack and Lily were riding on Tom, their magical unicorn.

Jack and Lily saw a dragon and the dragon started to save them.

The dragon made some fire so they ran away.

So they ran back to Tom. They told Tom to help them.

They flew to a rude witch. She didn't let them in the castle.

So Jack and lily took the broomstick and flew home.

Sarpreet Lidhar (6)
Hambrough Primary School, Southall

64

Vedant's Magical Tale

Jesika and Jacky had a pony ride on a lovely sunny morning. Jesika took her teddy called Freddy.

They arrived on a mountain. They were horrified by a fierce dragon, the dragon smoked fire out of his mouth.

They ran as quickly as they could to save their lovely lives.

They sat on their unicorn again. Then they set off on their journey ahead.

They reached Lolly Land and met a nice witch. This was her first time to meet someone and she gave presents of a lolly to teddy.

The witch offered her broom to Jesika and Jacky. They all had a nice day with the witch. At dusk they returned home on the witch's broom.

Vedant Bhardwaj (7)
Hambrough Primary School, Southall

65

Harpreet's Jungle Tale

Me, my sister and my teddy were swinging across the jungle.

We saw a snake looking like he wanted to bite us. We were very scared.

We started running to save ourselves. My teddy was running very fast.

Then we saw a big tiger. He had big eyes and big face. We were scared.

But he was very friendly. We sat on his back, he was running fast to save us from the snake.

After that we swung back home. We really enjoyed it in the jungle.

Harpreet Singh (5)
Hambrough Primary School, Southall

Joshua's Pirate Adventure

Once a boy called Sam and his sister, Zora went to find treasure.

They found it but they saw a pirate ship coming by.

A pirate told them off for taking his treasure.

He was angry so he made them walk the plank.

Luckily some dolphins came to the rescue.

And so they went home.

Joshua Samuel (6)
Hambrough Primary School, Southall

Bushra's Magical Adventure

Once upon a time there was a girl and a boy riding on a unicorn.

They saw an angry dragon throwing fire to them.

They were scared and ran away from the dragon.

They came back to the unicorn and they got onto it.

They came across a witch. The witch gave them a magic broom.

They came back with the broom and went to sleep.

Bushra Rahman (6)
Hambrough Primary School, Southall

68

Kenyngton Manor
Primary School
Sunbury on Thames

Ben's Space Story

In space Spencer, the elf, took Ellie to the moon to collect lots of shiny sparkly stars.

They were so busy that they didn't see a green alien swoop down behind them.
'Hello,' said the alien. 'Do you want me to take you home?'

'Can I come with you?' said Spencer, the elf.
'I can't see why not,' said the alien.

They went past Mars and saw a scary monster.

He tried to eat them but they went too high in the sky. Alien took Ellie home.

Ben De Costa (6)
Kenyngton Manor Primary School, Sunbury on Thames

Charlotte's Magical Adventure

There was a pretty unicorn, they rode it.

Then they saw a scary dragon!

It breathed fire at them then they ran to the unicorn.

They ran as quickly as they could go and she let them off.

Then they met a witch. It came out of its house and said, 'Go away!'

They went back home.

Charlotte Mann (7)

Kenyngton Manor Primary School, Sunbury on Thames

Trinity's Pirate Adventure

Suddenly the elf saw a pirate. Ellie did not see the pirate.

The elf saw Captain Hook, Ellie did not. She stood on a pirate treasure chest.

Captain Pete drew his pointy sword. Ellie's teddy was terrified!

The elf had to walk the plank. Ellie looked at the elf.

Soon dolphins rescued them. Riding dolphins with them *whooshing!*

Ellie went home, it was fun with the elf.

Trinity Emery (6)
Kenyngton Manor Primary School, Sunbury on Thames

Sophie's Magical Adventure

Once upon a time lived a unicorn, it was pink and the hooves were purple.

The unicorn was running. As the unicorn stopped there was a red dragon.

The red dragon followed, Spencer and Ellie followed too.

The first unicorn came back, they stopped at Sweetie World.

Sweetie World is white and colourful but there was a witch. She put a magic spell in her pocket and the pink unicorn was scared of the witch.

The witch saw them so they went home on her broomstick.

Sophie Sheldrick (6)
Kenyngton Manor Primary School, Sunbury on Thames

Sam's Zoo Adventure

At the scary zoo and Steven and Ellie went to wander around.

Afterwards then they had a look around they went on a large elephant to go to an exciting park.

They saw baby pandas. Steven held the baby panda and Ellie cuddled the panda.

They said bye to the pandas because they wanted to see the cheeky monkey.

So they trampled off to see the cheeky monkey. Steven and Ellie's teddy swung on the vines.

Ellie ate a banana with the monkey then it was time to go home the elephant brought Ellie home.

Sam Walker (6)

Kenyngton Manor Primary School, Sunbury on Thames

Jack's Space Story

Ellie was flying and holding's Spencer's hand.

Then they saw a green alien.

Then they flew to the land of the stars.

They waved to all the stars.

They saw a wiggly monster.

The alien flew away.

Jack Curran (7)
Kenyngton Manor Primary School, Sunbury on Thames

Tanya's Magical Adventure

Ellie and Spencer and the ted were going on an adventure to Fairy Tale Land.

When Teddy met a dragon the dragon said, 'I will eat you up!'

'No you won't!'
'Yes I will!'

So the dragon breathed out his flame but the dragon didn't get the children.

The children went home so that the dragon couldn't get them.

Then they met a witch and the witch said, 'Do kids like you want to go home?'

So they want home together on the broomstick and off they all went.

Tanya Spracklan (6)
Kenyngton Manor Primary School, Sunbury on Thames

Ruby's Space Story

In the starry sky above Earth, Ellie and the elf, Spencer, arrived at the giant scary moon.

On the way to the moon Spencer collected some shiny stars.

The cheeky alien laughed. The green alien took Ellie up. She could not fit!

Ellie and the green alien went home for dinner. Ellie invited the green alien for dinner.
'No I can't,' he said.

But on their way a huge, big, red alien tried to get them.

Ellie said, 'Go away!' Spencer and the green alien waved goodbye.
Ellie said, 'Goodbye Spencer.'

Ruby Gould (6)
Kenyngton Manor Primary School, Sunbury on Thames

Elisha's Magical Adventure

Ellie landed in an enchanting place where the sky was always blue.

Spencer gave a drink of water and the unicorn grew into a dragon blowing fire.

After that they ran and looked terrified. While they were running they came to a castle.

Next Spencer saw that the unicorn had turned into itself so they got on the unicorn.

Spencer saw a wicked witch who lived in a lollipop land.

Finally they rode home on their broomstick with Teddy attached to the end.

Elisha Coughlan (7)
Kenyngton Manor Primary School, Sunbury on Thames

Jamie's Magical Adventure

They got a unicorn. They went on the unicorn and had a ride.

They got off the unicorn and they saw a dragon. The dragon had long claws.

They ran away from the dragon. The dragon was medium and angry and started to blow out fire.

Next they went on a unicorn again and had another ride because they sat on their unicorn.

They saw a witch. The witch said, 'Give me the lollipops and I will give you my broomstick.'

They went on the broom and went home to bed so they could get some sleep.

Jamie Lee Billing (6)
Kenyngton Manor Primary School, Sunbury on Thames

Jamie's Magical Adventure

They arrived at the land where unicorns lived. They got on the unicorn.

'Oh look over there,' said Spencer. There was a dragon!

Ellie and Spencer ran away.

Ellie and Spencer got back on the unicorn.

Then there was a scary witch. The witch said, 'You two can ride on my broomstick.'

They went back home.

Jamie Patterson (6)
Kenyngton Manor Primary School, Sunbury on Thames

Rachel's Space Story

They arrived at space. Ellie was happy. Spencer said, 'Are you happy for I am.'

First they looked at the shiny stars. They did not know that someone was watching them.

'Come on my cosy spaceship, it is fast.'

Ellie and Spencer had a fun ride all together.

An evil slimy monster wanted to come up but Ellie panicked.

'Can you take me home?'
'Yes of course.' So Ellie went home.

Rachel Tam (7)
Kenyngton Manor Primary School, Sunbury on Thames

Lucy's Magical Adventure

In a magical land they saw a fluffy white unicorn.

When they flew on the fluffy white unicorn they saw a red dragon.

So they quickly ran off because they were scared of the dragon.

So they went back on the fluffy white unicorn.

They saw a witch, she said, 'Do you want my broom to go home?' 'Yes please.'

They flew home with the witch's broomstick.

Lucy Bradley-Sleet (6)
Kenyngton Manor Primary School, Sunbury on Thames

Ellie's Pirate Adventure

They arrived at a sandy beach; all they could hear was the ocean.

Ellie found some shiny treasure the teddy was wearing a crown.

A pirate spotted Ellie and Spencer and took them away.

The pirate made Spencer walk the plank. Ellie was scared.

But luckily some dolphins rescued them.

Next they walked home.

Ellie Mackenzie (7)

Kenyngton Manor Primary School, Sunbury on Thames

Alyssa's Jungle Tale

One day Ellie and Spencer were swinging on the green vines.

They saw a green snake. They were very frightened.

They ran away.

Then they saw a lion and then the lion said, 'Do you want to go home?' 'Yes please.'

They rode on the lion's back home.

And Ellie and Spencer swung on the vines once more.

Alyssa Clare Hannig (6)
Kenyngton Manor Primary School, Sunbury on Thames

Taylor's Pirate Adventure

They had arrived in a boat. They started to row until they got to an island it was called Ellie Island.

But just then Ellie said, 'Look in the sand, there is a brown dusty chest that's big. Yes!'

'That's my treasure chest!'
'Sorry we didn't know.'
'I think you did.'
'Honestly, we didn't know.'

'If you're not going to tell me the truth you will have to walk the plank.

Luckily two dolphins caught them. One was called Flipa, the other was called Rose. It was a bumpy ride.

'That was a long trip.'
'Yes it was.'

Taylor Berekis (6)
Kenyngton Manor Primary School, Sunbury on Thames

Libby's Magical Adventure

At a magical place they rode a unicorn.
'It was a bumpy ride,' said Ellie.

Ellie and Spencer met a red scary dragon. It breathed fire at Ellie and Spencer.

Ellie and Spencer ran away from the scary red dragon.

Ellie and Spencer got on the unicorn and rode away from the scary red dragon.

They met a wicked witch and the wicked witch let them ride on her broom.

Then Ellie finally got home and went to bed.

Libby Cate Mandeville (6)
Kenyngton Manor Primary School, Sunbury on Thames

Nathan's Space Story

Soon they arrived in space.

Look at all these stars, should I collect some?'

Suddenly a UFO zapped Ellie!

Now look at all this.

Suddenly an alien appeared.

She was home.

Nathan Bendall (6)
Kenyngton Manor Primary School, Sunbury on Thames

Abigale's Magical Adventure

On a pretty unicorn they were at a magical place.

They met a nasty dragon and it blew fire at them.

They ran away but the dragon chased them.

They got back on the unicorn and the pretty unicorn went up the hill.

Then they saw a scary witch. 'You can go on my broomstick.'

They got on the broomstick and flew home.

Abigale Akers (7)

Kenyngton Manor Primary School, Sunbury on Thames

Jade's Magical Adventure

They arrived at the pink unicorn and they went on the unicorn.

They saw a dragon on the way there and the dragon blew out fire.

Then they went to run away from the dragon.

They got back on the pink unicorn.

Then saw a witch and she said to the children, 'You can fly on my broomstick. Drop Ellie home.'

And she got dropped off in her window.

Jade Lee Pickett (7)
Kenyngton Manor Primary School, Sunbury on Thames

Nafisa's Magical Adventure

They arrived on the white unicorn and they flew to a scary dragon.

'Oh no, the dragon is going to put fire on us!' So they ran away very fast.

So they ran to the white unicorn.

They went to a witch's house.

Then the witch said 'Would you like to go on my broomstick?' 'Yes please,' said Ellie.

Then they flew home but they liked the adventure.

Nafisa Chowdhury (6)

Kenyngton Manor Primary School, Sunbury on Thames

90

Luke's Space Story

Ellie and the elf are flying to the moon.

They landed on the moon and a sneaky alien was sneaking up on them.

Another alien zapped them up into his spaceship.

They were having fun and they are having a race.

Another alien licked the spaceship.

They flew back home.

Luke Mitschke (6)
Kenyngton Manor Primary School, Sunbury on Thames

Ava's Space Story

Ellie is flying in the sky. She is having a great time, Spencer is too.

A sneaky alien peeked behind.

Then a ship sucked up Ellie. Ellie got sucked in the ship. She didn't think it was good.

They had a spaceship race, it was fun.

Then a monster came and tried to eat them.

Then they landed on Earth and went home.

Ava Blewett (5)
Kenyngton Manor Primary School, Sunbury on Thames

Amaan's Space Story

Ellie went to fly and they went flying off.

A sneaky alien and Ellie had a touch on her back.

A flying saucer tried to pick Ellie up.

They had a space race.

An alien tried to beat Ellie up.

She said goodbye, she went to Earth.

Amaan Huda (6)

Kenyngton Manor Primary School, Sunbury on Thames

Harry's Space Story

They liked flying.

They landed on the moon and the creepy alien came.

They got stuck by the good alien.

They were having a race.

The monster got them.

They flew back home.

Harry Burgess (5)
Kenyngton Manor Primary School, Sunbury on Thames

Benjamin's Pirate Adventure

Ellie is in the boat.

Ellie is on the treasure.

They are sad. The pirate wants the treasure.

They went to the pirate ship. Spencer the elf splashed in the water.

The dolphins helped free them and Spencer and Ellie went on their backs to go all the way home.

They went back home for dinner and went to put the pirate things away in the treasure box.

Benjamin Casserley (6)
Kenyngton Manor Primary School, Sunbury on Thames

Erin's Jungle Tale

He was swinging on the monkey branch.

He was worried about the snake.

They run scared.

A fierce lion.

He gave them a ride.

They went on the monkey bars.

Erin Green (5)
Kenyngton Manor Primary School, Sunbury on Thames

Frankie's Space Story

They were flying.

They were picking stars.

They got sucked up by an alien ship.

They had an alien spaceship race.

They zapped the alien.

They took Ellie back home.

Frankie Wakelam (5)

Kenyngton Manor Primary School, Sunbury on Thames

Tayla's Magical Adventure

They sat on a unicorn, they rode on the unicorn.

A big dragon, they were scared of the dragon.

They ran with the teddy bear.

They jumped on the unicorn and they click clocked away.

They saw a witch, she was mean.

They flew home.

Tayla Spenceley (6)
Kenyngton Manor Primary School, Sunbury on Thames

98

Dayleigh's Pirate Adventure

A tap at Ellie's window.

They wanted the treasure.

They wanted to go home.

They wanted him to fall off the boat.

The dolphins saved them.

They went home.

Dayleigh Ayton (5)
Kenyngton Manor Primary School, Sunbury on Thames

JJ's Magical Adventure

They jumped on the unicorn.

They got scared.

They ran away.

They got on the unicorn.

They got stopped by a witch.

They stole the broomstick and they went home.

JJ Janneh (5)
Kenyngton Manor Primary School, Sunbury on Thames

Rytansh's Space Story

They are landing in the moon for an adventure.

The aliens are sneaking behind the people.

The aliens are grabbing.

They are racing.

The monster is licking the saucer.

He went back to Earth.

Rytansh Mahajan (5)
Kenyngton Manor Primary School, Sunbury on Thames

Matthew's Pirate Adventure

Ellie and Spencer were going to the island.

They found treasure. The pirate looked through his telescope and saw them.

The pirate got to the island and said, 'It's my treasure.'

The pirate made Spencer walk the plank.

Spencer fell onto a dolphin and brought them back home.

Ellie, Spencer and the bear went home happy.

Matthew Murphy (6)
Kenyngton Manor Primary School, Sunbury on Thames

Frankie's Jungle Tale

At the jungle they were swinging on branches.

They saw a snake.

They ran because they were scared.

They saw a lion; they were scared of the lion.

They rode the lion.

And they rode home.

Frankie Vickers (5)

Kenyngton Manor Primary School, Sunbury on Thames

Kaylea's Zoo Adventure

Ellie and Spencer went to the zoo. They felt happy.

Ellie and Spencer sat on the elephant.

Elle and Spencer went to the panda. They cuddled and Spencer held a baby.

Ellie and Spencer went on the elephant.

Ellie was with the monkey, they ate a banana.

Spencer rode an elephant.

Kaylea Wells (6)
Kenyngton Manor Primary School, Sunbury on Thames

Shai's Magical Adventure

They went to go on a unicorn to see a dragon.

The dragon blew fire at Ellie and Spencer, they were afraid.

Ellie and Spencer ran. The dragon blew fire.

Then the unicorn came back then they flew up into the sky.

Then a witch appeared. The witch said, 'Do you want a lolly?'
'No,' said Ellie and Spencer.

They went home to bed.

Shai Ayton (6)
Kenyngton Manor Primary School, Sunbury on Thames

Jack's Jungle Tale

They swung on the vines to find some animals. They met a friendly snake.

They got blocked by a snake. Ellie and Spencer met a friendly tiger.

They ran away, they came to a gorilla. He said, 'Do you want to have a cup of tea?'

They met a friendly tiger. The tiger said, 'Would you like a ride?'

'Yes,' said the bear.

Jack Hosmer (5)
Kenyngton Manor Primary School, Sunbury on Thames

Ethan's Magical Adventure

They went to a magical land, they went on a unicorn.

They found a dragon, it breathed fire.

They ran away.

The unicorn took them to a witch.

They went and found a witch. The witch gave them a broom.

They went home.

Ethan Willis (6)
Konyngton Manor Primary School, Sunbury on Thames

Farah's Zoo Adventure

In a zoo they saw a giant elephant and then they got on the elephant and they saw a giraffe.

The teddy got on the elephant's trunk. They all got on the elephant and there were leaves and sticks.

They saw pandas, Spencer hugged the baby and Ellie gave the panda a cuddle.

They saw leaves and there were trees and teddy said hello.

They saw another animal and he was a gorilla and he gave a gorilla to Ellie and teddy was swinging on vines.

Then Ellie went home on the elephant, she said, 'Bye bye.'

Farah Khan (6)
Kenyngton Manor Primary School, Sunbury on Thames

Jamie's Pirate Adventure

They are going on their holiday.

The children find some treasure.

There is a bad pirate.

The pirate is pushing the children into the sea.

The children are on the dolphins to get away from the rough pirate.

The children are on their way home after a nice time.

Jamie Coulter (5)

Kenyngton Manor Primary School, Sunbury on Thames

Zachary's Pirate Adventure

Ellie said, 'Where are we going?'
Spencer said, 'You will wait and see.'

When they got to the island they found treasure.

A pirate came and took Ellie and Spencer.

Spencer was made to walk the plank.

They had a ride on a dolphin.

They went home.

Zachary Light (6)
Kenyngton Manor Primary School, Sunbury on Thames

Jiyar's Space Story

Ellie and Spencer.

They took the stars.

An alien took Ellie!

Ellie went for a ride in the spaceship.

Ellie and an alien saw a scary looking monster.

Ellie waved goodbye to the alien.

Jiyar (5)

Kenyngton Manor Primary School, Sunbury on Thames

Casey's Magical Adventure

Ellie and Spencer saw a horse.

Ellie and Spencer saw a dinosaur.

The dinosaur blew out fire.

Ellie and Spencer found the unicorn.

A wicked witch said, 'Would you like a lollipop?'

Ellie and Spencer went home.

Casey Willoughby (5)
Kenyngton Manor Primary School, Sunbury on Thames

Kiera's Space Story

Ellie and Spencer were flying.

Ellie and Spencer were collecting stars.

Ellie popped in a spaceship.

Ellie was looking out of the window.

A monster tried to get the spaceship.

Ellie went home and waved to the alien.

Kiera Akers (6)
Kenyngton Manor Primary School, Sunbury on Thames

Libby's Pirate Adventure

Ellie and Spencer are going to the treasure island.

Ellie and Spencer find some treasure.

A bad pirate tries to take the treasure.

Ellie and Spencer go on the ship.

They go on the fish.

In the morning they go back home.

Libby Newman (5)
Kenyngton Manor Primary School, Sunbury on Thames

Mason's Space Story

They flew to space.

Then they collected pointy stars.

Then an alien took Ellie but they were good aliens.

Then some bad aliens tried to take Ellie.

Then a monster nearly licked them with his long tongue.

Then they went to bed.

Mason Griffiths (6)
Kenyngton Manor Primary School, Sunbury on Thames

Jignya's Zoo Adventure

Ellie and Spencer went to the zoo.

They met an elephant and they sat on it.

They met a panda, Ellie cuddled it.

Ellie and Spencer sat on elephant's back.

Ellie ate bananas with a monkey.

Ellie said goodbye to the animals and Spencer.

Jignya Pathak (5)

Kenyngton Manor Primary School, Sunbury on Thames

Bailey's Space Story

Ellie and Spencer flew.

They collected blue pointy stars.

Some good aliens took Ellie, she was sad.

The aliens flew and some more aliens came.

The big alien tried to capture them.

They went home.

Bailey Williams (5)
Kenyngton Manor Primary School, Sunbury on Thames

Alicia's Jungle Tale

Ellie and Spencer went to the jungle. They saw a monkey hanging on vines.
'We are going to see animals.'

They met a snake. They said, 'Hello Snake, can you let us past please?'
'No, go away!' said the snake.

They ran away from the snake. They were safe and they met a lion.

'Look at the lion!' Spencer said.
'It looks big,' Ellie said.

A lion took Ellie and Spencer very far.

They went back home, it was lovely.

Alicia Young (5)
Kenyngton Manor Primary School, Sunbury on Thames

Jaime-Lee's Magical Adventure

When they landed they saw a unicorn, they went on the unicorn. They told the unicorn to stop. The unicorn stopped so they saw the trees and leaves.

They saw a dragon. They ran because the dragon blew fire.

They ran faster and faster until they nearly got caught by the dragon. But the dragon couldn't find them.

Ellie shouted, 'Unicorn!' The unicorn came. When Ellie said to the unicorn, 'Stop!' The unicorn stopped.

Then they saw a witch and the witch said, 'Would you like a lollipop?'

Ellie said, 'No.'
Spencer said, 'No'
But Teddy said, 'Yes.' Teddy ate the lollipop.

They flew on a broomstick then they want home.

Jaime-Lee Hayes (5)
Kenyngton Manor Primary School, Sunbury on Thames

Northwood College
Northwood

Jude's Magical Adventure

Ellie and Spencer and Teddy rode away on the unicorn.

They met a dragon. The dragon scared them away.

They ran away as fast as they can.

They got on the unicorn to escape the dragon.

They met a witch. She said, 'Come and have some cake.'

They were scared of the witch so they went on the witch's broom heading home.

Jude Dobe (6)
Northwood College, Northwood

Inika's Magical Adventure

They went to Magical Land. They met a kind unicorn and asked to let them ride on her back.

They saw an angry dragon. They ran and ran. Soon the dragon was tired.

They ran as fast as they could. The dragon gave up.

The unicorn came back and dropped them at the candy land where candy grows.

They met a witch who loved children. She gave them candy to eat.

She let them ride on her broom.

Inika Prakash (6)
Northwood College, Northwood

Arshya's Jungle Tale

So off they swung into the jungle.

And they saw Simran, the snake. He was dangerous so the teddy sneaked off to get help.

'Run, I found someone who can help us,' said Teddy because Simran was going to cast a spell on them.

They met Limo the friendly lion.
'Please can you help us?' asked Ellie.

Limo gave them a ride back to the vines.

And they swung back home.

Arshya Bommaraju (5)
Northwood College, Northwood

Zahra's Jungle Tale

In a beautiful jungle it was full of big plants and trees and very warm.

As they walked through; they met a snake called Paa who was Kaa's big brother.

Paa said, 'I haven't eaten for days!' Ellie and Spencer were so scared that they ran away fast.

Suddenly they saw a lion and thought that he was mean.
'Don't worry, I am not mean,' said the lion.

'Climb onto my back, I will take you home,' said the lion.

Finally they reached home. Spencer said bye to Ellie and Ellie said bye to Spencer.

Zahra Shah (6)
Northwood College, Northwood

Aasiyah's Magical Tale

They were in colourful magical fairyland.

When suddenly a fierce dragon with fire in his mouth scared them.

So they ran as fast as their feet could carry them.

A little while later they found their unicorn, Alice and rode to see the witch.

She had lollipop trees and she gave them her broomstick.

Ellie and Spencer then got onto the broomstick and flew back whilst their unicorn followed behind them.

Aasiyah Alloo (6)
Northwood College, Northwood

Kiyanna's Jungle Tale

In a jungle a friendly bear smiled as he swung on a vine and Ellie and Spencer did the same.

Laughing, they landed and came upon a snake who looked angry because they had woken him up.

They were terrified because they thought the snake was going to gobble them down, so they ran away.

Then they met a lion. They were so, so scared, but the lion smiled at them.

He said, 'Would you like a ride on my back?'
'Yes please.' So Ellie, Spencer and the bear climbed on.
'Yippee!' they cried.

Soon they were swinging back on the vines which took them safely home again.

Kiyanna Mistry (6)
Northwood College, Northwood

Sapthika's Magical Adventure

That night Ellie and Spencer climbed on the magic unicorn with the teddy.

When they were still going on the journey suddenly they saw a fierce dragon. They were so frightened. 'Help! Argh!'

They began to run away and the teddy ran as well. The fierce dragon was showing his fangs.

At last and phew, we're saved. Good that we haven't been killed by the dragon,' said Ellie.

They saw something strange so they began to see. 'Oh! Oh!' said Spencer, 'It's a wicked witch!'

Suddenly they saw a magical broomstick. Spencer said the magic words and they flew back home safely.

Sapthika Rameshkumar (7)
Northwood College, Northwood

Faaizah's Pirate Adventure

They arrived at a boat to rest because they were tired. After a long time they arrived at an island.

They saw a treasure box, Ellie stood on the box. Suddenly the elf saw a ship coming towards the island.

The pirate came out from the ship. He had a sharp sword and a funny dirty bear. He made them scarper.

The pirate let the elf and Ellie go on his ship and asked them to jump; in the sea because he wanted to get rid of them.

When the elf, teddy and Ellie jumped in the sea, kind dolphins came to rescue them.

Dolphin took them out from the sea. They had a happy journey home.

Faaizah Ahmad (6)
Northwood College, Northwood

Layla's Magical Adventure

In a magical land called Dragal, Ellie, Spencer and Teddy landed on a pretty pink unicorn named Rosy.

Suddenly they saw a dragon called Angry Pops. Ellie's teddy came alive by the dragon's fire burp.

As his burp got bigger the fire got bigger so Ellie, Spencer and Teddy ran to Rosy.

Rosy said, 'Don't worry; I'll take you to Witch's grotto. It's fun and full of witch pops.'

Teddy picked a pop and ate it up and then a witch came and scared Spencer.

But the witch was actually kind and let Ellie and Spencer on her broomstick to go home.

Layla May Kara-Isitt (7)
Northwood College, Northwood

Khushi's Pirate Adventure

One sunny morning there were two children in a rowing boat. Eva was twelve years old and her brother Joe, was ten years old.

They rowed to an island and found a large chest. Inside the chest were lots of gold coins. Joe was worried when he saw the big pirate boat coming towards them.

The children were scared when a fierce pirate came waving a sharp sword. One of his hands was a metal hook and one leg was wooden.

Eva and Joe were taken to the pirate boat and Joe walked off the gang plank when he saw two dolphins.

They waved to the dolphins who gave them a ride home.

They walked home safely and happily. Their mum said, 'Where did you get those pirate hats from?' They told her the story.

Khushi Radia (6)
Northwood College, Northwood

Fatemah-Zahra's Zoo Adventure

Ellie and Spencer went to the zoo. They saw an elephant pecking from the gate.

They had a ride on the elephant. Then they saw beautiful emerald leaves.

They saw a gigantic and a tiny panda, they all hugged.

The next thing they did was go to see the chimpanzee.

The chimpanzee swung down from the trees. He brought a banana for Ellie. Chimpanzees love bananas.

Ellie and Spencer had a wonderful adventure.

Fatemah-Zahra Merali (6)
Northwood College, Northwood

Kiana's Magical Adventure

They arrived at a beautiful meadow with candy flowers. Suddenly Spencer saw a unicorn.
'Let's take a ride, said Ellie.
'Okay,' said Spencer.

They got off and went for a walk. Then they bumped into a dragon, a green spiky dragon.

They ran and ran but the dragon was catching up. The dragon was about to catch Ellie but Spencer shouted, 'There's the unicorn!'

They got on the unicorn and galloped away from the fierce dragon.
'Let's get off the unicorn,' suggested Ellie. So they did.

Just then they saw a witch. 'I've got you now,' cackled the witch.
'Let us go!' screeched Ellie at the top of her voice.

'Only if you get me candy flowers.' So they got the candy flowers. After that Spencer took Ellie home.

Kiana Shelley Ward (7)
Northwood College, Northwood

133

Krisha's Jungle Tale

One bright sunny summer morning my sister and I were bored, we were wondering what to do. Suddenly we had a great idea, it was to wish on our wishing teddy bear to explore the jungle. My sister and I packed some food, water, hats, binoculars and cameras. The teddy bear magicked up a flying carpet and off we zoomed. On our way we passed bright green fields and beautiful countryside. A while later we saw the deep blue sea. Soon we flew over the Amazon rainforest. Soon we reached the jungle. Our teddy bear led us through the jungle. Just then we had a problem, it was there was a long flowing river with snappy green hungry crocodiles in it. My sister and I were terrified! A few minutes later I had a brilliant idea; it was to swing on the vines to the other side of the river.

Soon we were at the other side of the river so we carried on exploring. Next we heard a hiss in the trees. It was a dark green snake with brown patches. The snake was coiling round the branches. My sister was terrified it might bite her.

The snake slithered down the tree. Soon it started to chase us. We ran as fast as our legs would carry us.

A while later we saw a bush move. I tiptoed to it as behind it was a lion. I almost jumped out of my skin. The lion started to say, 'Don't worry I am sorry to scare you but I am a friendly lion, do you want to be my friend? I will take you for a ride on my back.'
I shyly said, 'Yes please.'

We hopped on his back, the lion took us for a ride. Soon it was time to go home, Teddy magicked a flying carpet again.

Soon we were home, we had a magnificent time in the jungle. We never forgot that day.

Krisha Patani (6)
Northwood College, Northwood

135

Anvi's Magical Adventure

It was a lovely and warm day when Ellie saw a unicorn. She rides on the unicorn with Teddy Bear and Elf.

On the way unicorn suddenly changed into a big red scary dragon.

Fire was coming out from dragon's mouth so Ellie, Elf and Bear got so scared and ran away from there.

They saw unicorn again so they were happy and jumped on his back and started to come back home.

Unicorn took them to a lollipop place and disappeared. While Bear was eating a yummy lollipop a witch came and asked, 'Who are you?'

Witch gave them her broom. They sat on that broom and flew away to home. It was night-time. They were happy.

Anvi Gupta (6)
Northwood College, Northwood

Isha's Space Story

Soon they arrived on a massive planet. It was a cold, dark night and the bright, yellow stars were shining on them.

Suddenly a red, slimy alien popped up. Next it quietly tiptoed up to Ellie and Spencer and said, 'Hello, my name is Aghgh.'

Aghgh brought his funny looking spaceship and Ellie and her brown, cute teddy bear were pulled into it.

The spaceship took them around the galaxy and Aghgh showed Ellie the different planets.

A fat, ugly monster appeared and stuck his long, green tongue out. Ellie was frightened so she stood behind Spencer, the elf.

Later that night they landed on Earth and Ellie returned home safely.

Isha Shah (7)
Northwood College, Northwood

Shéra's Zoo Adventure

Ellie and Spencer arrived at the zoo. However this was no ordinary zoo, it was a magical and friendly zoo. All the animals could speak.

'Welcome to our zoo,' said Tomy the red elephant. 'Would you like to meet my friends?'
'Yes please,' said Ellie excitedly. Tomy lifted them up and off they went.

Firstly they went to see Cuddles the panda bear and her baby. They were eating bamboo shoots. As Ellie was about to go, Cuddles gave her a big warm and soft cuddle.

Soon Ellie, her teddy Lulu and Spencer were on Tomy again. They were going to see Banana Splits the monkey.

When they arrived he was eating a banana, he loved ripe, squishy yellow bananas. He saw that Ellie was hungry and gave her a banana.

It was getting late so Tomy and Spencer took Ellie back home. Ellie waved goodbye and thought about her adventure.

Shéra Kaur Aurora (6)
Northwood College, Northwood

Asiyah's Pirate Adventure

Suzen and Tomy wanted to sail to the other side of the sea to find some treasure.

They found the treasure easily. They started dancing with happiness.

Just then a scary pirate with a hooked hand and sharp sword said, 'How dare you touch my treasure! Follow me to my ship!'

The pirate was so angry with them he said, 'That's it, walk the plank!' So they did.

They were scared, struggling to swim when all of a sudden they were in the air. The dolphin saved them!

The dolphins took them to dry land. They happily walked home.

Asiyah Merali Dewji (7)
Northwood College, Northwood

Keya's Jungle Tale

Ellie, Spencer and Ellie's teddy, Raymond, swung on vines like monkeys.

Soon they met a snake; they were scared of the snake.

Ellie, Spencer and Ellie's teddy Raymond were so scared that they started to run.

Once they saw a lion, they were scared, even Ellie's teddy. The lion smiled at them.

Then Ellie, Spencer and Teddy had a ride on the lion's back.

Then they swung on their vines back home.

Keya Patel (6)
Northwood College, Northwood

Sneha Li's Zoo Adventure

Soon they arrived at their favourite zoo where their friends lived.

Suzy told them to hop on her back because she wanted to take them to see a big surprise.

Emma the panda was very happy to have a child of her own. Ellie and Spencer were so happy to see the new born baby.

Suzy let them have a ride to see another friend called Lucy.

Ellie said, 'I'm hungry,' and then Lucy gave her a banana to eat.

After that Spencer and Suzy took Ellie home and Spencer said, 'Goodbye Ellie,' and she walked home.

Sneha Li Amin (6)
Northwood College, Northwood

141

Aarushi's Jungle Tale

Once upon a time there was a girl, boy and a teddy. They were called Lucy, Ben and Toto.

One day they got lost. They walked through the jungle. They stopped because they saw snakes.

They ran away from the python. The python was chasing them. At last, they got away from it.

While they were running they stopped because they saw a lion. Ben was scared of the lion.

The lion was kind, not like other lions. Lucy asked the lion, if he would give them a ride.

When the lion stopped they got off. They swung across vines when they got off. They could see their house!

Aarushi Dubey (7)
Northwood College, Northwood

Anjani's Magical Adventure

Soon they arrived at the woods, but it was a magical wood. There were fairies and unicorns living there.

The unicorn was bad. She took the children to a crazy dragon. He breathed fire out of his mouth and scared the children.

The children were so frightened that they ran away as fast as they could.

On their way, they found a compassionate unicorn. She said she would stay with them.

Just then they met a considerate witch. She gave them a liquorice sweet but the children didn't like sweets.

So the witch said, 'Because you didn't take my sweet, you can take my magical broomstick to fly you back home.'

Anjani Soni (6)
Northwood College, Northwood

Arya's Space Story

In space!

An alien thought they would be tasty for lunch.

He zapped them into his spaceship.

Soon they became friends.

The space monster stuck out a long tongue.

The alien saved them!

Arya Panchmatia (5)
Northwood College, Northwood

Alyssa's Magical Adventure

At Magic Land they saw a unicorn and it said, 'Jump on my back!' They took off.

They landed at an unusual place. There was a dragon and he said, 'Go away, this is my land!'

The dragon chased them and they ran as fast as they could. They were scared.

Ellie and Spencer saw the unicorn and they jumped on his back and flew away.

They landed on Witch Land. The witch gave them a lollipop to make them stay.

When the witch was not looking they took the broomstick and flew home.

Alyssa Amin (5)
Northwood College, Northwood

145

Maansi's Space Story

Just then there was a blue and green circle. 'What is it?' they asked Ellie.
'The Earth, we're in space!'

Soon an alien saw but he was jealous. Just then they were stealing stars.

So the alien was super jealous. To Ellie's great surprise she was gone!

Ellie was having so much fun she forgot the time. But she did have a new friend.

Then they picked up Spencer and an alien. The alien was going to eat them!

Ellie had to go so they dropped her off at home where she wanted to stay.

Maansi Kalirai (7)
Northwood College, Northwood

Chloe's Magical Adventure

They went to a magical fairy princess land.

They saw a bad naughty dragon.

They ran away from the naughty bad dragon.

They had a ride on the rainbow beautiful unicorn.

They saw a witch and the witch gave a lollipop to Ellie's teddy.

The elf took Ellie and her teddy back home.

Chloe De Alwis (5)
Northwood College, Northwood

Neeyati's Zoo Adventure

So when they got to the zoo, inside it looked fun and exciting.

They saw some dazzling elephants, there was a beautiful multicoloured elephant and he let them have a little ride.

Next they went to see the glamorous panda and they swapped things.

Back came the lovely elephant again and he gave them a tour around the zoo.

Before they went back home they had one more animal left which was a gorilla.

But it was time to go back home. Ellie was very disgruntled and upset but she knew she could return.

Neeyati Patel (7)
Northwood College, Northwood

Zainab's Pirate Adventure

They arrived on an island, a beautiful desert island. They were tired; they had a rest on the island and closed their eyes.

They woke up; they saw a chest of gold. Ellie felt very rich and a teddy bear was wearing a crown.

Then the captain jumped out of his ship and crossly said, 'What are you doing on my island?'
Ellie and Spencer said, 'Sorry.'

The captain was so very cross, that he made Spencer go on his plank and Ellie felt very sad.

Ellie also walked on the plank but two happy dolphins rescued Ellie and Spencer. They felt very happy.

The dolphins took them to their street and the dolphins went home. Ellie and Spencer went home. Spencer took the captain's hat.

Zainab Naeem (7)
Northwood College, Northwood

Anagha's Magical Adventure

At Magical Land it was day. They saw a unicorn and were amazed. They rode on the unicorn and had fun.

When it was night the unicorn became a dragon. They went, 'Yikes, run!'

They ran and ran, the teddy ran too.

It was day and the unicorn came again.
'Do you worry if it will change into a dragon again?' said a voice.

It was a witch! But she was kind. She gave some lollies and said, 'The unicorn turns into a dragon at night.'

The sun was setting so they rushed home on the witch's broomstick. Suddenly Ellie woke up and found she was dreaming.

Anagha Sreeram (5)
Northwood College, Northwood

Mili's Jungle Tale

Once upon a time Dora and her friends were swinging on the magical tree branch.

They went on a jungle adventure. They met a dangerous snake.

They were scared and ran away.

Then they met a lion. The lion smiled at them and said hello.

They all became friends and played together.

The magic was finishing and Dora and her friends had to go back home.

Mili Thakrar (5)
Northwood College, Northwood

Aamena's Magical Adventure

At Fairy Land they sat on a magic unicorn for a ride.

Suddenly they saw a wicked dragon, he sprayed fire out of his mouth.

Ellie and Spencer were so scared that they ran away and dropped all their things.

They sat on the magic unicorn again and rode off to the end of Fairy Land.

They were walking back home when they saw a wicked witch.

She said, 'I will magic you into toads!' They stole her broom and flew away.

Aamena Merali (5)
Northwood College, Northwood

Ameera's Magical Adventure

Ellie and Spencer rode on a unicorn. Ellie and Spencer loved unicorns.

Then Ellie and Spencer saw a dragon, it looked scary but the dragon was a friendly dragon.

They ran away first in case it was a scary dragon and the teddy showed them the way.

Then Ellie and Spencer found the unicorn that they rode on earlier on they rode on it again.

Then they found a nasty witch but they thought it was a nice witch but it was a nasty witch.

The witch left her broomstick on the side so they took the witch's broomstick and rode it home.

Ameera Haji (5)
Northwood College, Northwood

153

Francesca's Magical Adventure

They arrived on the lovely unicorn in a magical land.

They met a very fierce dragon.

And then they ran away very fast.

Spencer and Ellie landed on the magical unicorn who rescued them.

'Do you think she is a bad witch or a good witch?' said Spencer.

She was a good witch and gave them her broomstick to fly home.

Francesca Hawes (6)
Northwood College, Northwood

154

Elina's Jungle Tale

In the jungle they swung on vines and had so much fun.
'This is great,' said Ellie.

After a while they landed softly. To their great surprise they met a smiling snake.
'Hello,' he hissed.

The malevolent snake spat venom out of his mouth. Ellie and Spencer ran for it! They were so scared.

They ran straight into a lion.

'Oh no,' said Ellie.
'Don't worry, he looks kind,' said Spencer.
'I won't eat you,' said the lion.

'I'm Leo, hop on, I'll take you to the end of the jungle.' They told him about the snake. 'Yes, you are lucky Sam likes to eat humans for lunch!' said Leo.

'Good night Leo,' said Ellie. They hugged him and swung home. She got into bed and Spencer went back to the moon.

'See you again Ellie.'

Elina Patel (7)
Northwood College, Northwood

Ameeya's Magical Adventure

Ellie and Spencer flew on a unicorn. The unicorn was magic.

When they got there they saw a dragon. They were scared. The dragon had huge claws.

The dragon chased Ellie and Spencer. They ran and ran but the dragon was too fast.

Ellie and Spencer finally got back to their unicorn. They hopped on and flew away.

The unicorn stopped flying and landed. The unicorn landed because she had seen a house made out of sweets and also seen a witch.

When the witch had gone to get something they climbed onto the witch's broomstick and flew away.

Ameeya Lad (6)
Northwood College, Northwood

Ariana's Magical Adventure

They landed on a unicorn. They were happy that they didn't have a bumpy fall. She dropped them in a spooky place.

A dragon passed Ellie and Spencer thought that the dragon was bad but it wasn't.

So they ran and ran, the dragon stopped but Ellie and Spencer kept running.

The unicorn saw them, she ran towards Ellie and Spencer and they jumped on the unicorn's back. Then she dropped them in a land where sweets are offered.

A witch came out of a house. The witch saw Ellie and Spencer. Ellie saw the witch's stick. Ellie snatched the broomstick.

They jumped on and they took it home

Ariana Doshi (6)
Northwood College, Northwood

Simran's Magical Adventure

At the land of elves, Spencer introduced him and his best friend, the unicorn, to Ellie.

One day a dragon came. He was looking for some delicious food.

When he saw Ellie and Spencer, he immediately ran towards them and said, 'I will gobble you up.'

After running a mile their legs started to hurt. They were pleased to see the unicorn.

After riding for ten minutes they saw a witch. She had purple hair, green skin and black clothes.

As they all played hide-and-seek Ellie grabbed the broomstick and they flew back home.

Simran Varia (7)

Northwood College, Northwood

Annanya's Zoo Adventure

Soon they arrived at a zoo. It was a warm calm night. The sky was clear and the stars were twinkling.

A beautiful white elephant welcomed them into the zoo. The elephant looked very anxious.

He told Ellie about a new orphan baby panda that had come to the zoo and the baby was sad and very lonely because he was missing his mum.

The animals are worried about the baby so Ellie and Spencer have being called to help. Ellie takes down some magic bananas from her special tree.

She tells the animals to start spreading happiness all around the panda.

Soon the panda was looking joyful. He had eaten some bananas and made friends with the animals and now liked his new home. Ellie had done a good job.

Annanya Chopra (6)
Northwood College, Northwood

Laaibah's Zoo Adventure

The two friends went to the zoo. They saw a trunk peeping out.

It was a friendly magical elephant. He took them on a magical ride.

They met pandas. It was a mummy and baby panda.

'Look, something ahead!' said Elf.

'Look, it's a monkey!' Ellie wanted a banana too.

It was bedtime, Ellie had a fun day.

Laaibah Ali (5)
Northwood College, Northwood

Orley Farm School
Harrow

Tayzah-James' Pirate Adventure

They sailed on the sea and in the distance they saw a hot, wonderful island.

They arrived at the island and they found a gold treasure chest. 'Ellie!' Spencer shouted, 'there are pirates on the ship.'

'Stand still! You can't steal my golden treasure. Now you will walk the plank,' the pirate said.

But when Spencer went into the water, he didn't fall in the water! A dolphin saved him.

Then another dolphin came and saved them from the evil pirate and they escaped.

When they got back Ellie was tired and she went to sleep and they lived happily ever after.

Tayzah-James Thomas (6)
Orley Farm School, Harrow

Dimple's Space Story

Spencer and Ellie arrived in wide and gigantic outer space.

Ellie was amazed. She saw gold and yellow stars sparkling and glistening in the darkness.

Suddenly a spaceship appeared, the light went on and Ellie and her teddy were sucked into and enormous spaceship.

They were spinning round with the glittering stars. Ellie and Spencer felt dizzy but excited.

Suddenly they saw a disgusting monster, with three eyes and eight arms!

Then Ellie got extremely tired, so Spencer carried Ellie to bed.

Dimple Raithatha (6)
Orley Farm School, Harrow

Adi's Pirate Adventure

They went on a blue sailing boat to a hot sandy island.

Ellie and Spencer found a treasure box. They opened it and they found gold.
'Hooray!' they shouted.

They saw a smelly pirate.
'You have my treasure!'

'Now you have to walk the plank.'
'Waaah.'

Then two dolphins came and they landed on them.

Then they went home.

Adi Inpan (6)
Orley Farm School, Harrow

Josh's Zoo Adventure

'Wow! I love the zoo and Teddy loves it even more. Let's go and explore.'

They sat at the top of a giant elephant and then got back on their adventure. Teddy was swinging on the trunk.

While they were walking they saw a panda. Spencer tricked the panda. The panda was holding Teddy.

They went on another elephant. Teddy was strangled with the elephant trunk; it was long and huge.

Teddy was on a long branch and a chimpanzee came with a lot of big, yellow bananas.

Spencer and Ellie got back home and elephant and Teddy waved goodbye.

Josh Holloway (7)
Orley Farm School, Harrow

Haroon's Zoo Adventure

Ellie and Spencer magically appeared at the zoo.

The elephant asked if they wanted to have a ride.

He took them to visit Passion, the panda. He was cuddly and cute.

Then they had a wonderful ride on the elephant.

Next they decided to have a fun time eating a big, juicy banana with a cheerful chimpanzee.

Ellie went home to bed and went to sleep. *Zzz.*

Haroon Khan (6)
Orley Farm School, Harrow

Alexander's Zoo Adventure

Ellie was very excited to be going to the zoo.

They went to see the giant elephant; it had a very long trunk.

They met the black and white, playful panda; it had a very cute cuddly baby.

After that the elephant gave them a ride.
'It's so bumpy, I'm going to fall off!'

Then they went to see the hungry, big chimpanzee.
'Can I have some of your delicious bananas?'

Ellie was having lots of fun but was very tired. They decided to travel home on the enormous elephant.

Alexander Nester Gong (7)
Orley Farm School, Harrow

Anaya's Space Story

Spencer and Ellie arrived in outer space, it was big and dark.

They landed on the gigantic moon. Spencer and Ellie collected glowing stars.

A cheeky alien in a flying saucer took Ellie away. The golden stars shone around her.

Ellie drifted away in the flying saucer. It was a lovely sight. It was fun exploring.

Suddenly an ugly monster appeared, it had three red eyes.

They went away in the spaceship. Ellie went home. The shimmering moon shone brightly.

Anaya Khan (7)
Orley Farm School, Harrow

Jai-Sai's Pirate Adventure

Ellie and Spencer found a wooden rowing boat and they sailed down the long, blue river.

Ellie found treasure, but they were in trouble! Pirates were coming and Ellie wasn't listening!

The pirates were here and the pirate wanted his treasure or they would abandon them.

The pirates got Ellie and Spencer and then Spencer had to fall into the sea.

Ellie and Spencer jumped onto a dolphin and sailed home.

They lived happily ever after.

Jai-Sai Mehta (6)
Orley Farm School, Harrow

169

Hugo's Zoo Adventure

Ellie was very excited.
'Come on Spencer, let's go!'

'Can we see the big, grey elephant? Can we ride on it please Spencer?'

'Let's go and see the black and white panda. The baby panda is cute.'

'Is the elephant exploring?'
'I think it is. It's a bumpy ride.'

'What is the next animal?'
'Let's wait and see.'
'It's a chimpanzee. I love bananas.'

'It is time for my bedtime, bye Spencer.'
'Have a nice sleep, good night, it has been a brilliant day.'

Hugo Dorrian (6)
Orley Farm School, Harrow

Aaran's Space Story

Spencer and Ellie arrived in big outer space.

Spencer and Ellie were excited as they explored the planet Mars.

An evil alien captured Ellie. She was scared as she was taken into the flying saucer.

The stars were glowing around her as she spun deeper into dark, wonderful space.

Just then they saw an evil monster. He had a long, grey tongue and eight arms!

Ellie was tired and hungry, so they travelled home. She waved goodbye happily.

Aaran Notta (6)
Orley Farm School, Harrow

171

Zara's Pirate Adventure

They sailed on the blue, shining sea to a burning hot island.

They saw a wood, gold treasure chest.
Ellie said, 'Let's open it.'
'OK,' said Spencer.

They saw an angry, mean pirate.
The pirate shouted, 'Who took my treasure?'

Spencer finally lost all his hope and walked the plank.

They cheerfully had fun riding on the smooth, grey dolphins in the rough sea.

The dolphins took them home. Spencer and Ellie were so happy they were going home.

Zara Saad (6)
Orley Farm School, Harrow

Shayen's Pirate Adventure

Ellie rowed a rowing boat on the shiny, blue sea. They saw an island, they went to the island.

When they got to the island they found some gold.

The wicked pirate found the treasure on the deserted island. Ellie and Spencer were scared.

Poor Spencer had to walk the plank. He was scared and frightened.

When he fell into the water a dolphin picked him out of the water.

They went home and Ellie went back into her bed and went to sleep.

Shayen Vaid (6)
Orley Farm School, Harrow

Matthew's Zoo Adventure

Ellie was amazed. They went for a ride on an elephant, it went very fast.

They went through some very thin trees searching for elephants.

Spencer took the baby panda and the panda took the teddy.

They saw some enormous trees. They went through them very slowly and steadily.

They stopped for a break and they had a juicy, yellow banana each.

Spencer went for another ride on the elephant. Ellie went back home with the baby panda.

Matthew Hallam (6)
Orley Farm School, Harrow

174

Yusuf's Pirate Adventure

Ellie rowed a rowing boat on the shiny, blue sea until they found an island. They decided to have a look at the island.

'I spy a treasure chest,' said Ellie.
'Shall we open it?'
'Yes,' said Ellie.
'Let me open it,' said Spencer.
'No, not now, see, there's a pirate ship.'

'Please can we have our precious treasure or I will make you walk the plank.'

Suddenly Spencer was walking the plank, he felt scared and frightened.

Instead of landing in the sea he landed on a kind dolphin.

The kind dolphin took him back to land and went back home happily.

Yusuf Kundqol (6)
Orley Farm School, Harrow

175

Aryan's Space Story

Spencer and Ellie arrived in the wide outer space.
'This is wonderful!'

'Hmm, what shall I do with her? I know, I will kidnap her.'
'I am having so much fun.'

Suddenly a big laser zapped Ellie up.
'Help, Spencer!'
'I am coming.'

At first Ellie was scared, then they had lots of fun.

Suddenly they saw a huge monster. It had a long tongue, they zapped it up quickly.

Ellie was sleepy.
'Bye, I will see you again.'

Aryan Marde (7)
Orley Farm School, Harrow

Isabela's Magical Adventure

One day Ellie and Jill went on a magical adventure. They met a kind unicorn.

Suddenly a fierce dragon came. The children were frightened.

They ran as fast as the could because the dragon was breathing fire.

The unicorn came to save them. She took them to see a witch.

The witch was kind. She gave them lollipops and promised to help them.

The kind witch gave her broomstick to the children.

Isabela Asid (6)
Orley Farm School, Harrow

Shyan's Space Story

Spencer the elf and Ellie flew into dark, spooky space. They flew very fast.
'That was great.'

They landed on freezing Jupiter with a thump and a bump.
'Look, there's a giggling alien,' said Spencer.

They were caught by a spotty, scary flying saucer. In the flying saucer there were several buttons.

They flew higher and higher until they saw Teddy with an alien.

They passed an alien with three eyes.

When Ellie got home she said, 'Thank you.'

Shyan Shah (6)
Orley Farm School, Harrow

178

Khushi's Magical Adventure

One sunny day Khushi and Jill went to a magical adventure. Khushi saw a beautiful unicorn who took them to a sunny hill.

A fierce, horrible dragon crept near to Khushi and Jill. The flame of the dragon's breath was stinky and hot.

Khushi said, 'Run for your life!'
They ran so fast the dragon fell down.

The unicorn saved Khushi, Teddy and Jill's lives.

When they saw the witch she was really kind. They thought it was food. The witch gave them lollipops.

The children borrowed the kind witch's broomstick and flew home.

Khushi Raizada (6)
Orley Farm School, Harrow

Lukas' Space Story

Spencer the elf and Ellie flew into dark, shiny space. Ellie is holding her soft, rainbow-coloured teddy.

Finally they landed on snowy Mars. They saw an alien, his name was Ryan. They played all sorts of games and collected stars.

Ryan said, 'I'm going to take you in my sparkly, orange flying saucer.'

They flew higher and higher until they nearly reached the top of space.

Then they saw an alien with three eyes and he was hairy all over and he had 1,000 teeth.

They got home and when they went through the door her mum had baked a cake for them.

Lukas Hamilton (6)
Orley Farm School, Harrow

180

Kabir's Pirate Adventure

Ellie and Spencer found themselves in a big, colourful boat. The sun was beaming hot.

Then they reached the island. They found some treasure, they were excited.

A pirate called Rusty Old Leg, had returned for his treasure.
'I will kill you and I will shoot you with my gun!'

Captain Rusty Old leg took them to his pirate ship.

Suddenly the dolphins arrived to take Ellie and Spencer home.

'Thank you Spencer for a wonderful adventure.'

Kabir Sethi (6)
Orley Farm School, Harrow

Bradley's Space Story

Ellie and Spencer flew into the dark, shiny space. Ellie began to get excited.

They landed on Mars. Mars was freezing , they got colder and colder.

A nice alien came and zapped them into his flying saucer. The flying saucer was very fast.

They zapped every alien in its way.

They zapped the ugly squid out of the way.

The alien dropped Ellie and Spencer home.

Bradley Hodge (6)
Orley Farm School, Harrow

182

Ibrahim's Pirate Adventure

Ellie and Spencer were rowing in the boat, the sea was very calm.

They ended up on a beautiful island.

'We have found some treasure,' said Ellie.
'Get away from my treasure, you scurvy scum.'

The pirate took them onto his ship and then he made Spencer walk the plank.

Suddenly two dolphins appeared to rescue them.

Spencer took Ellie home after a busy day.

Ibrahim Peerbacos (6)
Orley Farm School, Harrow

Aarin's Space Story

Spencer the elf and Ellie flew into dark, shiny space. Ellie was holding her cuddly teddy.

They landed on Mars.
Spencer looked and said, 'That's where we live!'
Ellie saw an alien, it was very cute.

The cute alien went into his spaceship and took them up, up and up.
Ellie and Teddy were very scared.

They looked at the shining stars. They had a good time. The alien was very friendly.

Then suddenly they saw another alien. It had three eyes.
'That looks funny! Doesn't it look funny?'

Then they landed.
'Wow!' said Ellie.
They landed at home.
'Yay!'

Aarin Sharma (6)
Orley Farm School, Harrow

Anya's Space Story

Spencer and Ellie want to go to space where it is very dark and shiny.

They flew very fast and felt a bit sick.

They landed on Jupiter where it was very cold. They saw a cheeky, green, little alien.

The alien took Ellie and her cuddly teddy to Mars, flying in his blue saucer. They loved it.

They went a long way. Then suddenly they bumped into another alien's spaceship.

They saw a monster with sharp teeth and a long tongue.

Then they had to go to their small, dark house.

Anya Mittal (6)
Orley Farm School, Harrow

185

Oliver's Pirate Adventure

Ellie and Spencer arrived in a boat, they rowed on the calm, still, silent sea.

They sailed to Treasure Island. It was amazing! The treasure was sparkling.

They saw a pirate ship, it came closer and closer.
'Do not touch my treasure!'

Spencer had to walk the plank.
'Help!' he shouted, he was scared.

Suddenly a blue dolphin rescued him.
'I will get you next time,' said the pirate.

After Spencer had taken Ellie home she lived happily ever after.

Oliver Slade (6)
Orley Farm School, Harrow

Liam's Magical Adventure

One cold day Liam and Sheil saw a unicorn. She was kind and gave them a ride.

Suddenly Liam said, 'Help! It's a scary dragon, run for your life!'

They ran until they were far away from the dragon.

The unicorn saw them and gave them a ride to the wicked witch.

When they arrived they found a broomstick.

Then they flew home.

Liam D'Costa (6)
Orley Farm School, Harrow

187

Anaya's Space Story

Ellie and Spencer were rushing and zooming through the huge, dark night's sky.

They landed in a bright blue spaceship and they decided to catch stars. They did not see the alien laughing.

When Ellie was walking she saw a flash, luckily it was a friendly alien.

The alien took Ellie for a ride in his circular yellow and gold spaceship.

The alien, Ellie and Spencer saw a three-eyed alien, they felt very frightened.

The alien dropped Ellie home.
She said, 'Goodbye,' to Spencer and the alien.

Anaya Gohil (7)
Orley Farm School, Harrow

Jay's Space Story

Ellie and Spencer floated gently into big, dark outer space.

Spencer and Ellie were catching stars while a green alien was spying.

Suddenly Ellie was sucked up by a fantastic alien, flying a circular spaceship.

Another circular spaceship appeared behind them. Luckily it was friendly.

All of a sudden a red-tongued, green-eyed monster came.
'Oh dear,' whispered Spencer.

Spencer and the alien got Ellie home safely. Ellie was happy to be home.

Jay Raithatha (7)
Orley Farm School, Harrow

189

Dylan's Pirate Adventure

Ellie and Spencer are going to a hot island in a small brown rowing boat.

When Ellie got to the island she shouted, 'A treasure box!' Suddenly a pirate ship appeared.

When the swashbuckling captain came, he shouted, 'That is my treasure, I am going to make you walk the plank!'

Spencer was about to walk the plank when suddenly a dolphin appeared.

The dolphins gave Spencer and Ellie a ride across the ocean.

Spencer and Ellie are going home.

Dylan Ravindran (6)
Orley Farm School, Harrow

Shuruthi's Magical Adventure

Twinkleheart, the unicorn, took Ellie and Spencer to the most wondrous, magic adventure they had ever been to!

Suddenly a fierce dragon blew smoky, red fire.
'Run for your lives!' screeched Ellie.

The dragon was after them. Suddenly Twinkleheart flew through the thick smoke.

So they galloped back to town.
'Are we going home?' said Ellie.

But ...

A witch saw them. 'I am going to cast a magic to change you into frogs!'
So they made their only escape.

They snatched the hairy broom and flew back through the street.

Shuruthi Soruben (7)
Orley Farm School, Harrow

Dayan's Magical Adventure

Once upon a time there was magical unicorn and his name was Magic Kate. He lived in the world of Magic Land.

Suddenly a dragon appeared from a nearby bush. The dragon had very ugly, disgusting, big eyes.

'Run for your life!' shouted Ellie, 'Thank goodness for that.'

Then the dragon came running after them.

Then Kate came back again to take them somewhere else.

Kate took them to a kind, helpful witch.
The witch said, 'You're lucky young man and little girl.'

They went on a brown broom to go home.
'Thank goodness,' said Ellie, 'This is the end of our adventure.'

Dayan Pindoria (6)
Orley Farm School, Harrow

Kian's Magical Adventure

Once upon a time Ellie and Spencer the elf, found a white, sharp-pointed horned unicorn, his name was Helpful.

Then something bites the wing, it was a dragon and then the unicorn ran away. The dragon blew orange and red fire.

Then Ellie and Spencer ran away. The dragon followed them. Then the dragon stopped.

Then Helpful, the sparkly unicorn, came to help them.

A mean old witch came. Spencer did some good magic to make the witch good.

The witch let Ellie and Spencer borrow her old, black broom and they flew off into the night.

Kian Patel (6)
Orley Farm School, Harrow

Aadam's Space Story

Ellie and Spencer flew happily up into dark space from Earth.

Spencer grabbed sparkly stars. They did not see the laughing alien behind them.

Suddenly Ellie was sucked up by the alien's spaceship. She screamed loudly!

Luckily the alien was friendly and showed her all around the planets.

There was a three-eyed monster under the spaceship.

The spaceship dropped Ellie home quickly.

Aadam Sharif (6)
Orley Farm School, Harrow

Ranee's Space Story

Ellie grabbed Spencer's hand as he took her on an amazing adventure into big, dark, black space.

Spencer picked sparkly stars from the sky for Ellie. A cheeky alien was spying on them.

A kind alien sucked her up onto his spaceship. But Ellie thought the alien was kind.

Then the aliens said, 'Hello,' kindly.
Ellie was surprised.

A big, creepy monster was trying to get into the brown spaceship.

Luckily the monster did not get in. Spencer and Ellie waved as they dropped Ellie home.

Ranee Gudka (6)
Orley Farm School, Harrow

195

Sabeh's Pirate Adventure

Ellie and Spencer are rowing to Colossal Island.

Spencer and Ellie had reached and Spencer saw pirates in the sea.
Ellie had found a chest of gold.

A pirate comes. His name is Captain Skunkbeard.
The pirate said, 'That's my treasure.'

The pirate said, 'Walk the plank.'
'Why?' asked Spencer, but Spencer walked.

When Spencer fell down, dolphins came to help.

Ellie and Spencer lived happily ever after.

Sabeh Sahni (6)
Orley Farm School, Harrow

196

Arjun's Space Story

Ellie and Spencer floated gracefully through vast, wide space.

They were too busy catching silver, sparkly stars to notice an evil alien laughing.

Just then the scared Ellie was sucked up by a mean, nasty alien.

The alien growled wickedly, 'Do you see this dark, wide space? I am the space police, I drop all the space intruders home.'

All of a sudden a googly, three-eyed monster was about to lick them up, but the alien thought quickly and put the beam down.

Ellie was dropped home swiftly by the speedy police spaceship and she fell fast asleep.

Arjun Rajkumar (7)
Orley Farm School, Harrow

Iman's Magical Adventure

Ellie wanted to go on an adventure.
Spencer said, 'You can ride on my purple unicorn.'
'Wow I would love to.'
'His name is Sparklehorn.'

Suddenly a big fire-breathing dragon pranced right in front of them.
Ellie didn't say a word because she was so frightened.

Ellie shouted, 'Run for your life!'
The dragon was right behind a steep hill.
'Phew!' said Ellie.

Finally they came to a safe place but they didn't see the witch who was peeking from behind the bushes.

But the witch said, 'One chance. Take my broomstick, then you can fly on it to your home.'

They whizzed on the broomstick right to Ellie's house.

Iman Darr (6)
Orley Farm School, Harrow

198

Aaron's Pirate Adventure

It is a hot day, the boat is brown. Spencer and Ellie are rowing to a hot island.

Ellie gets her spade out and finds treasure on the island. A pirate ship is behind.

'Give me your treasure!' said Captain Aaron.
'No,' said Ellie.
But the pirate wanted the treasure.

Captain Aaron took Ellie and Spencer with him. He made Spencer walk the wooden plank.

When Ellie and Spencer jumped off the plank blue dolphins jumped up and saved Spencer and Ellie.

Ellie and Spencer went home.
'That was a good adventure,' Ellie said.

'That was!' said Spencer.

Aaron Kibria (6)
Orley Farm School, Harrow

Shanil's Pirate Adventure

Suddenly Spencer and Ellie were sailing in a silver, shiny boat towards a deserted island.

Ellie found a box, which was full of gold money. The pirate ship was behind them.

The pirate ship had arrived, and the pirates were stealing the treasure box. They were stealing Ellie and Spencer too.

The pirates took the treasure box and made Spencer walk the plank.

Up jumped two dolphins. Spencer and Ellie were saved by the beautiful blue dolphins.

Then the dolphins took Ellie and Spencer safely home. They were wearing pirate hats.

Shanil Vora (6)
Orley Farm School, Harrow

Rafae's Pirate Adventure

Ellie and Spencer found themselves in a big, colourful boat. The sun was burning hot.

Then Ellie and Spencer found themselves with a golden, sparkling treasure chest.

Then an angry looking pirate called Captain Blackbird appeared right in front of them.

He shouted, 'You scallywags don't get my treasure!'

Then Spencer had to walk the plank and said, 'Help me Ellie!'

Suddenly two dolphins came to help them. Ellie and Spencer were really happy.

Spencer took Ellie home and Ellie said, 'Goodbye.'

Rafae Shafi (6)
Orley Farm School, Harrow

St Michael & St Martin's Catholic Primary School
Hounslow

Analiza's Zoo Adventure

At the zoo the elephant welcomed them.

Then the elephant gave them a ride. They saw something in the bamboo.

It was the mummy panda and her baby panda. Ellie hugged the mummy panda.

Then the elephant gave them another ride.

They visited the gorilla and ate some bananas.

The elephant dropped Ellie back home.

Analiza Fernandes (6)
St Michael & St Martin's Catholic Primary School, Hounslow

Melissa's Zoo Adventure

They arrived at the zoo. Jumbo was waiting for them.

They rode through the bamboo trees.

They met Mrs Panda and Baby Panda.

They walked through banana trees.

A gorilla offered Ellie a yummy banana.

Soon it was night and Ellie had to go home.

Melissa Andrews (5)

St Michael & St Martin's Catholic Primary School, Hounslow

205

Oscar's Space Story

They flew high above the stars. Ellie was amazed at the stars.

They landed on a small planet. Spencer started to pick up some stars.

Then a spaceship arrived and took them in. Ellie was shocked at the alien.

The alien's name was Tom and he was very friendly. He showed Ellie his world.

On one planet lived a monster, he was very nasty.

At the end they arrived at Ellie's home. She will never forget this trip and her new friends.

Oscar Dudzinski (6)
St Michael & St Martin's Catholic Primary School, Hounslow

Tristan's Pirate Adventure

Billy dreamed he was on a boat with his sister Emma.

They landed on a desert island with lots of treasure.

An angry pirate appeared with a big sword.
He said, 'Get away from my treasure!'

The pirate took them to his ship and made them jump into the sea.

Luckily two dolphins were passing by and rescued them.

Billy and Emma were pleased to be home.

Tristan Brown (6)
St Michael & St Martin's Catholic Primary School, Hounslow

Edela's Zoo Adventure

Once there was a little girl who met an elf with wings.

Afterwards they went on a fun ride on an elephant.

They were expecting to see a panda and guess what? They did meet a panda.

Then they had a slow ride by the same exciting elephant.

Before the story finishes she had a snack from a kind monkey.

The elf went back to its exciting home and the little girl did too.

Edela de Villiers (6)

St Michael & St Martin's Catholic Primary School, Hounslow

208

Hayley's Space Story

Ellie and Spencer were having a trip to the moon to catch some stars.

Suddenly they landed and caught some stars. Whilst they were doing that an alien came.

The alien took Ellie and put her in his spaceship. Ellie felt nervous.

Ellie was not afraid of the alien, they actually made friends.

When they were flying they found Jack and a giant alien.

After a while Spencer and the alien took Ellie home.

Hayley Mae Garcia (6)
St Michael & St Martin's Catholic Primary School, Hounslow

Nathan's Space Story

'Wow, this is amazing!' said Ellie as they whizzed past a long road of millions of sparkling stars in the sky.

They landed safely on the moon and reached the stars. An alien had been watching.

Then the alien lifted up Ellie to his spaceship. Ellie felt very nervous because she did not know what was going on.

Next, Ellie and Spencer were taken to Planet Mars. Ellie though the spaceship was very shiny.

After that they landed on Planet Mars. They saw a purple monster. He was very lonely, they made friends with him.

Finally, Ellie had to go home.
Then Ellie said, 'Goodbye,' and waved to them.
What a great adventure!

Nathan Bowman (6)
St Michael & St Martin's Catholic Primary School, Hounslow

Shamika's Magical Adventure

When they got there they met their friend, Uly, the unicorn.

Suddenly a dragon swooped down. Ellie and Spencer felt frightened.

The dragon breathed even worse. The flames got thicker. They ran off.

They ran and ran until they could run no more. Then they found Uly.

Soon Witchy, the witch, wanted to make a spell on Ellie.

Finally Ellie caught the witch's broomstick and flew home.

Shamika Fernando (7)
St Michael & St Martin's Catholic Primary School, Hounslow

Maya's Pirate Adventure

One day an elf took a girl for a ride in a yellow boat.

They saw a yellow and golden treasure box. The girl jumped on the box.

A pirate came and he was angry with the girl. He opened the treasure box.

They pirate told them to put the treasure box in the boat and he let them go.

The girl and elf had a ride on a dolphin. They were happy.

The elf took the girl home and they were happy again.

Maya Goraczynska (6)
St Michael & St Martin's Catholic Primary School, Hounslow

Tiara's Space Story

One little girl was with an elf high above in amazement. The little girl had her teddy with her.

One funny looking alien saw the little girl and the elf looking at bright, yellow, twinkling stars.

The funny looking alien went into his spaceship and got the girl and they teddy into it with him.

The girl and the alien made friends, so the girl stayed in there with him.

Because it was so dangerous to stay down there the elf went in the spaceship. They were attacked by a weird monster.

Sadly the girl and the teddy had to say goodbye to the alien and the elf.

Tiara Niklekai (7)

St Michael & St Martin's Catholic Primary School, Hounslow

Jed's Pirate Adventure

Two children, called Sam and Emily, were on a boat and saw an island.

They found a big chest full of gold coins.

A big pirate came and took them with the treasure chest.

He made them walk the plank.

Two dolphins rescued them and took them ashore.

Finally they found their home.

Jed Fernando (6)

St Michael & St Martin's Catholic Primary School, Hounslow

Melanie's Jungle Tale

The children were swinging through the green trees on vines.

They came across a python that wanted to hug them.

If the python did hug them he would crush them and eat them. The children ran away.

The children came across a friendly, happy, yellow lion.

The children went on the lion's back and they had a rocky ride.

The children went on the green vines. They went home to see their mother.

Melanie Southey (7)
St Michael & St Martin's Catholic Primary School, Hounslow

Joshua's Zoo Adventure

One fine day Ellie went to the zoo with her friend Spencer.

They had an elephant ride and they enjoyed it.

They met sweet, cuddly pandas and Ellie hugged the mummy panda.

'What a lovely day,' said Ellie while riding on the elephant.

Ellie said, 'Yummy!' while eating a banana next to the monkey.

Ellie said, 'Bye-bye, see you next time.'

Joshua Cabucos (5)
St Michael & St Martin's Catholic Primary School, Hounslow

Alisa's Space Story

Spencer took Ellie into outer space, far, far away from Earth.

They landed on an alien planet. Spencer showed Ellie the twinkling stars while an alien spied on them.

The alien asked Ellie if she wanted a ride in his spaceship. Ellie agreed but she was a bit scared.

Ellie enjoyed the ride, she saw lots of different planets and stars.

They saw a scary and funny creature on Mars, with a big and sticky tongue.

Spencer and the alien dropped Ellie back to Earth. Ellie wished that she could go again.

Alisa Aurangabadwala (6)
St Michael & St Martin's Catholic Primary School, Hounslow

Gizelle's Pirate Adventure

They reached an island on a boat.

There they found a treasure box full of gold.

But to their surprise there was a rude pirate.

He captured them and took them on his ship.

Then they found their old friends, Chi-chi and Mi-chi the dolphins.

They came to their rescue and they got back home safely.

Gizelle Furtado (5)
St Michael & St Martin's Catholic Primary School, Hounslow

Joan's Magical Adventure

Once there was Kate and Bet, riding the horse and they were having fun on the horse.

But then they met a dragon and they were scared of the dragon and he blew fire.

So Kate and Bet ran as fast as they could to get away from the dragon.

So then they kept travelling on the horse and speaking together.

But suddenly there was a witch and Kate and Bet were looking very nervous.

So Kate and Bet flew off on the witch's broom and they could see their house.

Joan Arackal (6)
St Michael & St Martin's Catholic Primary School, Hounslow

Riyana's Space Story

Once upon a time there was a girl called Ellie and her friend Spencer.

Spencer and Ellie went on an adventure that had lots of aliens.

They were on a strange planet but Spencer wasn't there, only Ellie and her teddy.

Then Ellie became friends with the aliens and took a ride in their spaceship.

On the way back home Ellie saw Spencer waiting with a mysterious monster.

Then the alien and Spencer dropped Ellie and Teddy back home.

Riyana Manangan (6)
St Michael & St Martin's Catholic Primary School, Hounslow

Kacper's Zoo Adventure

Spencer, Ellie and a little bear arrived at the zoo.

They saw an elephant and they rode on it through the zoo.

Then they saw a panda bear with a baby and they touched it.

Again they had a ride on the elephant. They really enjoyed it.

Then they went to the monkey and they had some bananas.

After the adventure at the zoo, Ellie and Spencer went back home.

Kacper Lepko (6)
St Michael & St Martin's Catholic Primary School, Hounslow

221

Raiden's Pirate Adventure

Once upon a time there were children who were sailing on the sea.

They found treasure.

There was a pirate.

The pirate was rude.

The children rode home on a dolphin.

The children said, 'That was a real adventure!'

Raiden Human (6)
St Michael & St Martin's Catholic Primary School, Hounslow

Olivia's Jungle Tale

They arrived in the jungle swinging the ropes with Ellie's little teddy bear.

When they jumped off the ropes a slimy snake slithered up to them.

Unfortunately the ugly snake chased Ellie and Spencer the elf.

They ran and ran as fast as they could until ...

Guess what? They saw a friendly, furry lion. At the very beginning they were a little bit frightened but not for long. The lion kindly took then to the place they wanted to be.

At last they reached the ropes. While they were swinging they looked at the small, pretty house.

Olivia Latka (7)

St Michael & St Martin's Catholic Primary School, Hounslow

Theresa's Jungle Tale

One day Ben and Katy were playing in the jungle with their teddies. Ben's teddy was named Zack and Katy's teddy was named Rose.

Ben and Katy decided to explore. On their way they met a poisonous snake.
The snake said, 'I will make you poisonous!'

They were so frightened they hit the snake with a branch and ran away.

Later they met a huge smiling lion and asked if the could have a ride on the lion's back.

The lion said, 'Yes, of course you can, I am friendly.'

The lion took then back home and they played on the swings happily ever after.

Theresa Kandathil (6)
St Michael & St Martin's Catholic Primary School, Hounslow

Ranah's Jungle Tale

At Candyrain Forest they met Billy Bear, Spencer's friend. They were swinging on liquorice strings.

They met Slippery Snake eating gummy trees.
'Hello friends, do you want to have s-s-supper?' slithered Snake.

Billy Bear then ran away. Suddenly he started screaming. When Ellie and Spencer got there they saw Lionel Lion.

Ellie told Lionel that they were lost and asked if they could ride him to the end of Candyrain Forest.

It was getting dark so Billy Bear, Spencer the elf and Ellie all went and had a nice cocoa at Ellie's house.

Ranah Akua Stoiber (6)
St Michael & St Martin's Catholic Primary School, Hounslow

Britney's Space Story

Once upon a time there lived a boy and girl. The boy was not an ordinary boy, he had wings.

The boy took his sister to another planet. Then Alien Pom-Pom thought he could destroy Earth.

While his sister was getting sucked into the spaceship her brother went exploring in the deep, dark holes.

Alien Pom-Pom let the children wave goodbye to their friends and family.

As they were flying across the universe the long-tongued blob caught them.

Next, after nights and days they finally got back to Earth safely.

Britney Sen Dias (6)
St Michael & St Martin's Catholic Primary School, Hounslow

226

Kyle's Space Story

So they grabbed her teddy and they flew off to another world.

Then they went to a planet to collect some stars, but something was watching them.

The alien brought them to the spaceship.

Before long they were racing in their spaceship through the stars.

The green monster nearly grabbed them with his long, sticky, red tongue.

Finally the alien brought Ellie and Teddy home. What a fun adventure they had.

Kyle Ferrer (5)
St Michael & St Martin's Catholic Primary School, Hounslow

Jayden's Magical Adventure

They had gone for an adventure on a horse ride.

They met a dragon and they were very frightened.

They started running as fast as they could.

Soon they were on the horse riding through.

On their way they met a witch, she gave them a lollipop and the magic broom.

They sat on the magic broom and flew away back home happily.

Jayden Rodriques
St Michael & St Martin's Catholic Primary School, Hounslow

Matthew's Magical Adventure

Ben and Sam went off on another adventure with their friend Dazzle.

They were having lots of fun when suddenly they bumped into a mean dragon.

They turned and ran away as quickly as they could. The dragon chased them.

From nowhere Dazzle appeared.
She said, 'Jump up and I will save you!'

Soon they bumped into a wicked witch who changed Dazzle into a broomstick.

Ben and Sam jumped on the broomstick and rode home.

Matthew Childs (6)

St Michael & St Martin's Catholic Primary School, Hounslow

Kenneth's Space Story

Spencer took Ellie to space near the moon and the stars.

The aliens on the moon saw Spencer and Ellie.

The aliens took Ellie and Spencer on their spaceship.

Ellie, Spencer and the aliens went across the stars and had fun in the spaceship.

They fought with the space monsters and beat them.

The aliens and Spencer then took Ellie to her home.

Kenneth Fernandes (6)
St Michael & St Martin's Catholic Primary School, Hounslow

Abigail's Space Story

Once upon a time there lived a fairy. He took a girl into space with her teddy.

An alien looked at them. He thought he might take them for an adventure.

The alien beamed them up into his spaceship.

They had lots of fun in the alien's spaceship.

They saw monsters with long tongues and three eyes and with one hundred legs.

They took the girl back home and the boy and the alien had so much fun again.

Abigail Dunn (6)
St Michael & St Martin's Catholic Primary School, Hounslow

Charlayne's Jungle Tale

I swung on a tree with my friends, it was fun! I was bored so I went to see something more interesting.

I saw a gigantic snake, my heart started pounding. We were all frightened, we stood still. It hissed at us so we moved one step back.

We ran for our lives until we found somewhere to hide.
I said, 'Quick, over here!'

In the bush we saw a lion hiding.
We asked the lion, 'Are you hiding?'
The lion answered, 'No, I'm not!'

So the lion gave us an exciting ride to escape from the jungle.

We got home just in time for dinner.

Before we went home we said, 'Thank you lion.'

Charlayne Tetteh (7)
St Michael & St Martin's Catholic Primary School, Hounslow

Aleksandra's Magical Adventure

Eva and Sam had a friend, Ben. One day, they met in a garden, a nice unicorn, Dotty. They played together.

The kids saw a scary dragon. Eva and Sam were afraid because he had long claws and sharp teeth.

The dragon started to blow fire from his mouth. Eva, Sam and Ben ran away as fast as they could.

Then they jumped on Dotty's back to escape from the dragon to a safe place.

The kids found lollipops in a field. When Ben tasted it, a witch came. She asked angrily, 'Why are you eating my sweets?'

The witch wanted to catch them but clever Sam grabbed the witch's broomstick and everybody went back home happy.

Aleksandra Makowiec (6)

St Michael & St Martin's Catholic Primary School, Hounslow

Keshiya's Zoo Adventure

Once upon a time there lived a boy and girl. They both went to the zoo.

When they were at the zoo the boy and girl climbed on the top of a very big elephant!

Then they cuddle with the baby panda and the big panda, near the bamboo.

Then after that they went on an elephant again. They were exploring the jungle with the bear.

After that the girl met a gentle gorilla that was eating a yellow banana.

Then the boy came to drop the girl to her house. They lived happily ever after.

Keshiya Fernando (7)
St Michael & St Martin's Catholic Primary School, Hounslow

Matthew's Space Story

Jed the elf and Tiara are flying in space.

Then they land on the moon, an alien spies them.

The alien leaders take them on an adventure.

They fly around the universe.

Then a space monster appears in front of them.

Then they drop Tiara off at home.

Matthew O'Neill (6)
St Michael & St Martin's Catholic Primary School, Hounslow

Anna's Zoo Adventure

The girl and boy are going to the zoo.

They are going on an elephant on their way.

They meet a polar bear on their way.

The elephant is holding a little monkey.

The little girl is eating a banana with the gorilla.

The boy is going to send the girl to her home.

Anna George (6)
St Michael & St Martin's Catholic Primary School, Hounslow

Carlos' Space Story

One night, Ellie and Spencer went flying to space on a space rocket.

They landed on the moon. They picked stars from the black sky along the way. They didn't notice that there was an alien looking at them.

The alien had a spaceship too; he used gravity to lift Ellie up to the spaceship.

Before Ellie realised, she was in the spaceship with the alien and they were flying through outer space.

They saw a bigger alien nearby, but they flew away from it.

Finally, the alien friend brought Ellie's home.
They all said, 'Goodbye.'

Carlos James Cabillan (7)
St Michael & St Martin's Catholic Primary School, Hounslow

Jennifer's Zoo Adventure

Jake and Katty went to the zoo to see some amazing animals.

They met an enormous elephant.
He said, 'Let's go and see my friend, Patch, the panda.'

Patch had just had a beautiful baby. Jack held it just like a teddy bear.

Eric, the elephant, took the children to see the mischievous monkey.

Mike, the monkey, gave Katty one of his delicious bananas to eat and they ate together,

After their wonderful day at the zoo, Eric took Jack and Katty home.

Jennifer Zerkhfaoui (6)
St Michael & St Martin's Catholic Primary School, Hounslow

Alric's Pirate Adventure

It was a very sunny day and pirates were rowing their boat to get to the island where there was treasure.

The children found precious, gold treasure in a box on the island.

A big, fierce pirate came to the island and he said, 'Give me that gold treasure.'

The big pirate and the children sailed to Dolphin World where the dolphins were diving.

At Dolphin World the children had lots of fun and had a good adventure with the dolphins.

Finally they reached home safely and were happy ever after.

Alric Costa (6)
St Michael & St Martin's Catholic Primary School, Hounslow

Chloe's Space Story

Spencer and Ellie decided to go to the moon.

When they got there they caught some stars and an alien laughed at them.

Then the aliens took them to their spaceship.

When they got inside they waved goodbye.

But when they were coming back to Earth they saw a horrible monster by the way.

Then they flew back to Earth. Ellie realised that it was just a dream.

Chloe Penelope Marie Deocampo (6)

St Michael & St Martin's Catholic Primary School, Hounslow

St Michael's CE
Primary School
Enfield

Yekta's Zoo Adventure

Soon the arrived at the zoo in Wonderland and were greeted by a giant elephant called Jugels.

They were on a ride with Jugels visiting the animals in the zoo.

They stopped by baby panda and her mum to feed them bamboo sticks.

They carried on their journey towards the trees.

Ellie was eating a banana with a cheeky monkey while they were resting.

Ellie was returned home safely by Elf and Jugles. Ellie went back to her bedroom to bed.

Yekta Kivanq Soylu (6)
St Michael's CE Primary School, Enfield

Matthew's Space Story

They floated around in outer space and landed on a meteorite.

An alien saw them collecting stars.

The alien zapped them up into his spaceship.

They twirled around in space looking for baddies.

When they found a baddy they zapped into it.

After all the zapping they took Ellie home.

Matthew Ryan (5)
St Michael's CE Primary School, Enfield

Ella's Magical Adventure

They arrived at Magical Land on a pink unicorn. They were very happy.

But then a big, green, scary dragon blowing fire appeared.

Spencer, Ellie and her teddy bear were so scared they ran away as fast as they could.

Then the pink unicorn came back to rescue them.

They arrived in Lollipop Land where the met a kind witch.

The kind witch let Ellie, Spencer and Teddy ride home on her broomstick.

Ella Stylianou (5)
St Michael's CE Primary School, Enfield

Kai's Pirate Adventure

From their boat they could see a pirate's island. It was sunny.

They found some treasure that was by a tree.

The pirate was angry they found his treasure.

He put them on his boat and made them walk the plank.

Dolphins came to save them.

They went home together with pirate hats on.

Kai Sears-Tisbury (5)
St Michael's CF Primary School, Enfield

Nicola's Pirate Adventure

Ellie and Spencer were on the sea when they saw a little island.

When they went there they found a treasure chest. Spencer saw Pirates.

The pirate went there and took the treasure and took them on his boat.

Then, when they saw the dolphins they jumped off the boat.

They both rode on the dolphins on the way back home.

Spencer and Ellie were happy about their adventure.

Nicola Kovaci (6)
St Michael's CE Primary School, Enfield

Daniel's Magical Adventure

At the magical land there was a unicorn waiting to give them a ride.

Then they saw a dragon that breathed fire.

Ellie and Spencer and little teddy got scared and ran away.

Then they took the unicorn again at the magical land.

Ellie and Spencer got lost. A witch stopped them!
'Where are you going?' she said.
'We want to go home,' they said.

'You can take my broom,' she said.
So they flew all the way back home.

Daniel Negru (6)
St Michael's CE Primary School, Enfield

Aziz's Space Story

In space, 'Wow! It's real space,' said Ellie, 'I love it.'

'Spencer, look at the stars up in the sky.'
It was nice.

Ellie and Spencer went out of the spaceship and jumped up and down.

Ellie went on a spaceship with an alien.

'Cool!'
There was an alien with a big tongue.

'Bye Spencer.'
'Bye Ellie.'

Aziz Dalibalta (5)
St Michael's CE Primary School, Enfield

Louise's Magical Adventure

They got on the magic horse, which took them on an adventure.

On their way to the adventure they saw a dragon that scared them.

The dragon ran after them because he wanted to eat them.

Luckily the dragon did not get them. So they ran off.

The witch stopped them on the way.

Finally they found their way home.

Louise Buyoya (5)
St Michael's CE Primary School, Enfield

Emma's Magical Adventure

Ellie and Spencer arrived at a magical place riding on a unicorn.

A dragon appeared from the forest.

Ellie and Spencer were scared by the dragon.

The unicorn rescued Ellie, Spencer and Teddy from the dragon.

On their way, they met a witch dressed in black. They asked her for help.

The witch gave her broom to Ellie, Spencer and Teddy.

Emma Malo (6)

St Michael's CE Primary School, Enfield

Charlie's Space Story

They were flying to Mars to see the stars.

'Look at the stars,' Ellie.

Then there was a bright light.

Ellie and Spencer were taken by the light.

It was a UFO, flying through the stars.

'Look down below, there is a purple alien.'

Ellie spotted her house, so Spencer took Ellie home.

Charlie Henry (5)
St Michael's CE Primary School, Enfield

Pemi's Zoo Adventure

Spencer took Ellie on a special adventure to the zoo to meet different animals.

Fletcher, the elephant, took them on a tour round the zoo to look at different animals.

Ellie saw a big panda who told her a story of him trying to climb a tree with banana peels on his feet.

Spencer pointed at the insect on the leaf for Ellie to see.

Ellie enjoyed lunch with Boozu, the monkey, who told her the history of bananas.

Ellie had a busy day, Spencer dropped her home wishing her sweet dreams.

Pemi de-Dravo (6)

St Michael's CE Primary School, Enfield

Luca's Space Story

... on the moon! They were far away from our planet.

Ellie and Spencer were catching the stars. The alien was watching them.

The alien took Ellie in his spaceship.

They were flying.

Then they took Spencer too. 'Ohh!'

There was a big alien sticking his big tongue out to get into the spaceship.

Ellie was back home.

Luca Musca (5)
St Michael's CE Primary School, Enfield

253

Theo's Zoo Adventure

At the zoo Ellie was a bit scared.

The elephant cheered her up by letting her ride on his back.

They went to see Panda and he loved Ellie's teddy.

'Oh no! There is a tree,' said Spencer.
They ducked.

Ellie was hungry, so a monkey gave Ellie a banana.

Ellie went home, not forgetting to say thank you.

Theo Chapman (5)
St Michael's CE Primary School, Enfield

Radhesh's Pirate Adventure

They found a boat and rowed towards a nearby island.

Ellie was ecstatic about their find, but Spencer warned of an oncoming pirate ship.

The pirate was cruel and captured Spencer, Ellie and the treasure.

He took them aboard his ship and made them walk the plank.

Luckily they were rescued by two dolphins.

As they walked home Ellie thanked Spencer for an exciting adventure.

Radhesh Mistry (6)
St Michael's CE Primary School, Enfield

Robert's Jungle Tale

In the jungle they swung on vines.

They met a snake.

The snake chased them.

They saw a lion.

He took them for a ride.

They swung back home.

Robert Mitchell (5)
St Michael's CE Primary School, Enfield

Albert's Jungle Tale

In the jungle, swinging on the trees.

They met a snake.

They ran from the snake into a lion.

The lion had a disk round his head.

The lion gave the kids a ride back to the trees.

The kids went swinging back to their house.

Albert Shepherd (5)
St Michael's CE Primary School, Enfield

Billy's Zoo Adventure

At the zoo.

They met Nelly, the elephant, she took them for a ride.

They went to see Poppy the panda.

Nelly took Ellie and Spencer to see George, the monkey.

He gave them bananas.

Nelly took Ellie home.

Billy Cooper (6)
St Michael's CE Primary School, Enfield

Sonia's Jungle Tale

When they got there they swung on a branch.

They met a snake, he was frightening. They ran away.

They fell off the branch, but landed safely.

A lion lived close by.

He took them for a ride back to where they started.

They swung back home.

Sonia Speight (5)
St Michael's CE Primary School, Enfield

Ava's Magical Adventure

... at a magical land they jumped onto a shiny, calm unicorn.

They saw a fierce dragon, Ellie and Spencer were worried.

The ran really quickly because the fierce dragon was after them.

Luckily the calm unicorn took them away from the fierce dragon to a safer place.

Ellie and Spencer looked worried but she was a kind witch.

The witch gave Ellie and Spencer the broomstick to take them all the way home.

Ava Wynter (5)
St Michael's CE Primary School, Enfield

Daniel's Space Story

In space, on a planet called Danmog.

They loved being so close to the stars. But there was a bad alien watching them.

A good alien shone a bright light and lifted them into a space cube.

They flew around space, enjoying the view of the stars.

They were scared of the bad alien, but they were safe in the cube.

Finally Spencer and the good alien took Ellie back home. They waved goodbye.

Daniel Mogaji (5)
St Michael's CE Primary School, Enfield

261

Tommy's Magical Adventure

They had arrived in wonderful Magical Land and they galloped on a pinky-blue unicorn.

Suddenly there was a dragon.
'What's that?' said Ellie.

'It's a dragon, run!'
Spencer, Ellie and Teddy ran as fast as they could.

They were glad to find the unicorn, he had been having lunch in a castle.

Just then a wicked witch came along. Spencer and Ellie had had enough of Magical Land.

They pinched the witch's broomstick and flew all the way home.

Tommy Emery (5)
St Michael's CE Primary School, Enfield

Jack's Pirate Adventure

They found a boat and went across the lake to an island.

Then they were on the island and Spencer said, 'Look, there is a ship.'

A pirate came to the island saying, 'Arr, arr!' with his sword up!

One the ship the pirate said, 'Aye, aye maties.'
He made Spencer and Ellie walk the plank.

Then two dolphins caught Spencer and Ellie and they went for a jumpy ride.

Then they went home that night and they lived happily ever after.

Jack Brand (6)
St Michael's CE Primary School, Enfield

Kate's Magical Adventure

Ellie, Spencer and Teddy arrived in Magical Land on a unicorn.

They saw an enormous dragon, with orange flames coming out of his mouth.

Ellie and Spencer ran away like cheetahs from the dragon.

They got back to the unicorn and flew to meet the evil witch.

Ellie, Spencer and Teddy spoke to the green, evil witch.

When the witch was not looking they snatched her broomstick and flew home.

Kate Connolly (5)
St Michael's CE Primary School, Enfield

264

Ben's Magical Adventure

They arrived at a magical land.

They bumped into a green dragon.

Ellie and Spencer ran away from the dragon.

Then they met a unicorn.

The unicorn took them to meet a good witch.

She gave them a broomstick to fly home.

Ben Evans (5)
St Michael's CE Primary School, Enfield

Beth's Jungle Tale

In the jungle Ellie and her teddy, called Rachel, swung on vines.

They saw a snake. He was making a *hiss, hiss* noise and Ellie was scared.

They ran away. Spencer helped. They ran, but then they saw a lion.

The lion looked happy.
'We can be friends,' he said.

They had a ride on the lion. They had so much fun.

Then they had to go home, they went to bed and had good dreams.

Beth Warburton (5)
St Michael's CE Primary School, Enfield

Kaya's Jungle Tale

In the jungle they were swinging across a gooey snake river on the tree vines.

They landed next to a snake called Jake.

Jake the snake was trying to eat them.

Aslan came along, he was friendly and helped them get away from Jake.

Ellie and Spencer got on Aslan and rode off.

They crossed the tree ropes again, because Spencer the elf's house was where they would be safe.

Kaya Karabeyaz-Cowling (6)
St Michael's CE Primary School, Enfield

Vikasita's Magical Adventure

They came to the magical land. They met a unicorn, who gave them a ride.

A dragon gave them a fright. It started to blow fire.

Ellie, Teddy and the elf ran away.

The unicorn gave then a ride through the woods.

They met a witch and asked if she would lend them her broom.

Ellie and Spencer flew on the broomstick.

Vikasita Joshi (6)
St Michael's CE Primary School, Enfield

Max's Pirate Adventure

At dawn they came to Captain John Claws' treasure island.

There they found a chest of treasure.

But the mean captain caught them.

He made them walk the plank.

Luckily two dolphins gave them a ride.

Home at last! What an Adventure!

Max Lange (5)
St Michael's CF Primary School, Enfield

Ruby's Jungle Tale

Ellie, Spencer and Teddy swung on the vines.
'Wheee!' said Ellie.

Then they came to a big snake. They were worried.

The snake opened his mouth, *'Hisss!'* he said.
They ran away.

Ellie, Spencer and Teddy bumped into a lion. They were a bit scared.

But he was a friendly lion. He gave them a ride on his back.

They said goodbye then they swung on the jungle vines all the way home.

Ruby Gibson (6)
St Michael's CE Primary School, Enfield

Frankie's Space Story

Ellie and Spencer flew over the stars.

They saw an alien. He was their friend. Tom was his name.

Tom sent them down to Mars. They saw animals.

Then Ellie got into the alien's spaceship.

'Oh no, there's a monster, we need to go!'

Spencer and the alien took Ellie home.

Frankie Jones (6)
St Michael's CE Primary School, Enfield

Sam's Zoo Adventure

They got to the zoo and met an elephant.

The elephant carried them up to the panda.

The panda was happy to see them. Ellie had a cuddle.

The elephant carried them to the monkey.

The monkey gave them a banana.
Ellie said, 'Yum!'

The elephant waved goodbye. Ellie had good fun.

Sam Ross (5)
St Michael's CE Primary School, Enfield

Ed's Space Story

They reached space. It was amazing. The moon was really made of cheese!

They collected some shiny stars. But an alien was watching.

Ellie was going up. She looked up, it was an alien flying saucer.

They were blasting away. Ellie felt happy until ...

Suddenly a bad octopus stuck his big tongue out to catch them. The bad octopus alien missed.

They dropped Ellie off at home and waved goodbye.

Ed Hathaway (6)
St Michael's CE Primary School, Enfield

Ben's Jungle Tale

In the jungle ...

Spencer, Ellie and Ted swung on the vines, until ...

They met a snake who hissed at them and told them he was king.

They were all scared and ran away quickly.

They met Mr Lion who was kind and he took them for a special ride.

Mr Lion showed them all around the jungle.

They said goodbye.
Spencer said, 'I think Mr Lion is the real king of the jungle.'

Ben Jones (6)
St Michael's CE Primary School, Enfield

Harry's Space Story

They arrived in space. It was exciting and fun.

Spencer caught some stars. The alien had a nice plan.

He wanted to give Ellie a ride in his spaceship.

They flew all around the galaxy looking at the stars and planets.

On one planet they saw a scary alien. It tried to lick the ship.

They dropped Ellie at home. They all waved goodbye.

Harry Phillips (5)
St Michael's CE Primary School, Enfield

Young Writers
Information

We hope you have enjoyed reading this book - and that you will continue to enjoy it in the coming years.

If you like reading and creative writing drop us a line, or give us a call, and we'll send you a free information pack.

Alternatively if you would like to order further copies of this book or any of our other titles, then please give us a call

or log onto our website at **www.youngwriters.co.uk**

Young Writers Information
Remus House
Coltsfoot Drive
Peterborough
PE2 9BF
(01733) 890066